YAZIR AND NINA
A CALIFORNIA HOOD ROMANCE

A Novel By
SHVONNE LATRICE

Published by Leo Sullivan Presents
www.leolsullivan.com

Prologue One: Nina Joy

"Lay down with me some more." Phillip kissed all over my neck and collarbone.

We were in his room, chilling like we always did every day this summer. It was around 7:30pm at night, and I was gonna meet up with my best friend for something important.

"I'm gonna be back in a little while, babe," I giggled and nudged him off of me.

"Alright, you better," he said as he watched me stand up and button my jeans. "I love you, Nina," he bit his lip.

"I love you too, baby."

Forty-five minutes later...

I sat on my best friend's toilet, staring at the positive pregnancy test in my hand. I was only sixteen years old, and I had no job or mind to take care of a baby. I didn't believe in abortions though, so I would have to find a way to get used to the idea of being a mother.

KNOCK!

KNOCK!

"Hurry up, Nina!" my best friend Aubrie screamed outside the bathroom door.

"Okay!" I shouted back and pulled myself together.

I washed my hands and then stared into the mirror. I'd seen this scenario in plenty of movies, but I never thought it would happen to me. I was not the girl who got pregnant before she was married, or before the age of twenty-five. What would my mother say? She had so many dreams for me to live out, and I knew I couldn't do that if I became a mother at sixteen.

BAM! BAM!

"Alright!" I grunted. She was really pissing me off! I yanked on the door and brushed past Aubrie, with the test clutched in my hand.

"What does it say?" Aubrie stared at me sympathetically as if she wasn't just rushing me out of the bathroom.

"I'm pregnant," I showed her the test.

"Damn Nina, now what?" She looked into my eyes. I stared back into hers, and then nibbled on my bottom lip in hopes of keeping my tears at bay. "Don't cry!" Aubrie pulled me into a hug and squeezed me tightly. I broke down and buried my face into her shoulder. "Nina, it's gonna be okay. You have to tell Phillip, though," she caressed my head.

"I am." I pulled out of her embrace and grabbed my jacket.

Phillip had been my boyfriend for the past year, and he was a great guy. I loved him so much and he loved me, but I wasn't sure how he would feel about me having his baby.

I met Phillip while at a party one night, and we'd been attached at the hip ever since. My mom disapproved of him, because she said he was a pedophile. He was seventeen at the time, and I was fifteen. I didn't care what she said though, and I'm still happy about my decision to this day.

"You want me to come?" Aubrie smiled and I shook my head no.

"I'll be good," I sniffled. I rushed out of Aubrie's apartment, and ran the whole way to Phillip's house.

The cool air felt good, and kept me from getting sweaty and hot from running. As I neared his home, I saw it was surrounded by police and ambulance trucks.

"What the..." I said to myself as I slowed down but kept towards the ruckus.

"Stay back, young lady," one of the officers blocked me.

I looked over his arm, and saw E.M.T.'s coming out of Phillip's house, rolling multiple bodies zipped up. My heart started to beat fast, and I had a huge lump needing to be swallowed.

"Phillip!" I screamed and didn't care if I yelled in the officer's ear.

"What happened, sir? Please tell me! This is my boyfriend's home!" I cried to the officer. He was an older black man with salt and pepper hair. He shook his head at me, and then dropped it.

"Someone came in and murdered the young man, his sister, and mother," he said to me and my heart dropped. I felt like I was on a rollercoaster taking a deep plunge.

"Nooooo! God! I was coming right back!" I hollered as my vision became clouded with tears. "Nooooo! I shouldn't have left!" I screamed and almost dropped to the ground, but the officer caught me. "Phillip!" I cried and tried to run after the ambulance truck, but the officer grabbed me. That murderer just took away the love of my life. Everything seemed to be spinning in circles. Please tell me this is a dream, I thought. "Wake me up!" I yelled as the officer held me up. My legs were no good at this point.

"Young lady, how old are you? Shouldn't you be home?" he asked me. I ignored him as I sobbed violently. "Where do you live?" he asked me again, but I continued to cry. He took me to his police vehicle, and then sat me in the passenger seat. He talked to his fellow officers, and then came to get in on the driver's side. I was still crying and my body was sore from jerking so hard.

"Young lady, I need your address so I can drive you home."

"Philliiiipppp," I cried and banged on the dashboard, before dropping my head into my hands. Why was this happening to me? And right when I find out I'm pregnant.

***

I cried for weeks for Phillip. I cried so hard and long that I lost our child. My mother was outraged when she found out I was pregnant, but I didn't care about the backlashes I received. I felt like nothing worse could happen to me now that my love was gone.

At the funeral, I was a mess. I cried loudly the whole time, and everyone looked at me like I was crazy. I wasn't embarrassed at all, though. I loved that boy and nothing or no one could ever stop me from showing my passion for him.

Apparently, his sister helped robbed some gang bangers, and the dudes came back and retaliated on the whole family. I tried hard not to hate Phillip's sister, Persia, but it was very hard. She was always getting into trouble, and Phillip was always bending over backwards to get her out of it. I remember his own mother would tell him that Persia was gonna get him harmed one day. He didn't care though, because that's just how great of a guy he was. He would give the shirt off his back if you needed it, even if it meant he might freeze to death without it. I felt for Phillip's mother too, because she was so worried that Phillip would lose his life over Persia, that I'm sure it never crossed her mind that she may lose hers too. I shook my head at my thoughts as I let my tears fall where they may.

I was lying in my bed, which was located under my window, just staring at the wall. I was thankful that it was summertime, because that meant I didn't have to get up everyday and apply myself in class. Also, I didn't have to deal with people asking me what happened, if I was okay, and all that crap. I just thank God that the only people who knew of my pregnancy were my mother and Aubrie.

KNOCK! KNOCK!

"Come in!" I shouted and waited for my mother to enter my room.

"Baby, aren't you hungry?" she inquired.

"No," I responded in the lowest tone possible. My appetite had died right along with Phillip, and just like him, it wasn't coming back.

I felt her hand on my back, and she began to rub it slowly. "Nina, honey, sit up," she said. I exhaled, but not too heavily, because I didn't want to disrespect my mom. I sat up and looked down at her kneeling in front of my bed. "Nina, I know you loved Phillip, but he wasn't good for you. He was eighteen years old sleeping with a baby. Now, I want you to shape up, put that beautiful smile on that pretty face, and get ready to accept the great things life has to offer you. When you get a little older and more mature, a better man will enter your life Nina, and that love will last forever," she half smiled and kissed my cheek.

"I should've stayed with him like he asked," I whimpered.

"If you did, you would've been dead too. Now stop saying that," she stated angrily. That would've been okay with me, I thought.

"Okay, Mom," I replied just so she would leave.

I believed none of what she was saying, because the man that was my soul mate was in the ground. No matter how many years passed, no new man would compare to Phillip.

"Now, I made your favorite food tonight, along with some rice pudding with extra cinnamon like you like. Did you want me to bring it to you?" She placed her hand on her hip.

My mother was a thick, fair-skinned woman, with long hair down to her tailbone. We looked just alike except for I had skin the color of milk chocolate. People always asked if I was mixed with Indian or something because of my extremely long hair. They asked me so much, that in kindergarten I asked my mom to tell me what I was mixed with so I could let the kids at school know. She asked me why I wanted to know, and when I told her, she explained that people were ignorant and to let everyone know I was just a regular old black girl with long hair.

"I'd like to eat in my room," I finally answered my mom. She nodded and then turned to get my plate.

In my eyes, the good life was over, and I was gonna have to find a way to make do.

Prologue Two: Yazir

In another world, some years later...

This was the last job of the day, and I couldn't wait for this shit to be over. I was tired as hell and my back was killing me like a muthafucka.

I wasn't built to work for the man. I was the type to work for myself. I had never done so before, but I knew I was destined to be my own fucking boss.

"Come on man." My co-worker, Johnny tapped my shoulder and then climbed out of the truck.

Currently, I worked for Greenyard Moving Company, and this shit was not the business. I was tired of dealing with heavy ass furniture, and indecisive ass muthafuckas who didn't know where they wanted their shit placed. I hated that we primarily worked in uppity ass neighborhoods, because everyone was so entitled, and they especially looked down on you when you were a black man. Black men were like plagues in these areas, unless you ran across a bored Caucasian housewife who wanted a good dick down session.

Johnny and I walked up to the front door of the house, and he rang the doorbell. I stared off into the street watching cars drive by, and I spotted a nice ass G-Wagon. I shook my head because that should be me. Matter fact, it would be me driving that shit soon. Yeah, I was only seventeen, but I had a dream. My mom said a man with a dream is better than a man with a regular old nine to five in some cases. She said a man would work harder for his dream than he would at his desk job, and it would always be more beneficial in the end. She was right, because I was gonna shed blood, sweat, and tears to make sure my dreams came true.

"Hello, Mrs. Lionel, is it?" Johnny asked the young white lady that answered the door.

"Yes, are you guys from Greenyard?" she beamed and we both nodded.

We had on uniforms that said Greenyard, what the fuck did she think? Calm down Yazir, I told myself.

She unlocked her screen door, and then stepped out to let us in. When we walked in, the house was a fucking mess. There was shit everywhere and she was clearly not in a position to move yet.

"We aren't too prepared right now, but just get what you can," she waved her hands in the air. See what I mean? Waving us off like she was the fucking Queen of England or some shit.

"Can you help us clear off the couch, though?" I questioned. I was trying my best to be respectful, but this job was running me low.

"No, that's your job," she shot me a fake smile and turned her back to me.

"Actua-" Johnny tapped my chest lightly to stop me from going in on this bitch.

Johnny was thirty years old, and needed this job to feed his family. He had a wife and five kids, so he was making sure to be the best employee he could be every damn day. I felt bad for people like Johnny, because they had to rid themselves of their pride in order to be able to provide for their families. This job meant everything to people like Johnny. They lived and breathed by it, and I would be damned if I lived like that at his age.

In my case, I needed this money just to feed my brother and myself, because my mama didn't have it. I knew if she could provide for us she would, but she just couldn't pay bills and buy food. As for my father, he's down in Mississippi with his new wife and family.

My brother, Sameer was two years older than me, but he couldn't find a job worth shit. It was hard getting employed when you were a young black man, because we were so heavily stereotyped it was ridiculous. His biggest problem was his dreads, because every employer wanted him to cut them and he always refused.

By saying that, money was scarce around the Willis household. The fact that I made $10 an hour was like a gold mine to Sameer and my mom. I was the breadwinner to say the least.

Johnny and I started to clear off the couch and the computer desk, so that we could move this heavy shit out to the truck. An hour and a half later, the living room was clear of the big furniture, so Mrs. Lionel had us go to the bedroom to start on it.

"How much is it if all of this takes longer than four hours?" she quizzed and threw her blond hair over her shoulder.

"It's $125 per hour that we go over, ma'am. So if we go two hours over, that would be $250-" Johnny responded.

"I don't need you to add it up for me sweetie, I can count," she rolled her eyes before walking off. "Marion, they said an extra $125!" she yelled to Mr. Lionel. I shook my head at Johnny, and he laughed as we started to clear off the bed.

These muthafuckas hadn't prepared shit for us to move, and then wanted us to pack stuff as well. This always happened over in these nice areas. I loved when we went to the hood, because Blacks and Hispanics would be ready to go. I wasn't sure if it was because they were organized, or because they didn't wanna pay the overage. Whatever the case was, they had their shit together. These white folks just wanted to kick back and watch us sweat.

"Which one of you pocketed my son's Wii controller?" Mrs. Lionel came running into the bedroom, just as Johnny and I were lifting the mattress.

"Uh, ma'am, neither one of us pocketed anything," Johnny frowned and then looked at me.

"Yeah, I packed the Wii box, but I saw no controllers around," I shrugged and she scowled. What the fuck am I gon' do with just a Wii controller? I would be better off stealing the system, and buying a controller since it's cheaper.

Mrs. Lionel turned on her heels and then switched off. Four hours later, we were done putting as much shit on the truck that would fit, and dropping it off at their new residence.

"Wasn't so bad, right?" Johnny smirked as we walked into the building to get our belongings from the locker.

"Willis, let me talk to you," my boss Bobby stopped me as I was going into the locker room.

"Sure, what's up?" I asked as I followed him to the office. He didn't respond, and once we reached his office door, he opened it for me to walk in and sit down.

"Willis, what happened at the Lionel's residence?" he quizzed, and folded his hands under his chin. He was an old fat white man, who was always red and greasy. He always coughed loudly as fuck, and he never covered his mouth.

"We moved the stuff," I chuckled nervously.

"What happened with the electronic device that was missing?" he squinted his eyes.

"I have no idea. Like I told the lady, I only packed the Wii, and saw no controllers around," I explained.

Bobby nodded and then reached into his file cabinet. He pulled out some paperwork, and then closed the drawer. "Willis, you know stealing is grounds for automatic termination, so I'm gonna have to let you go," he pursed his lips.

"What? I didn't steal anything! I just told you what happened, man! I need this job, Bobby!" I shouted.

"Look, it's either lose the business or lose you, and I'm sorry but Greenyard is more important than you." He slid the papers over for me to sign.

"I ain't signing this shit!" I shot up out my seat and yanked the fuck out of his door so that I could leave.

I went to get everything out of my locker, and then went home. As soon as I got to my apartment door, I saw an eviction notice addressed to my mom. I snatched it down and then went inside. This could not be happening right now. I didn't know what the fuck I was gonna do. Without this job, I was gonna go back to sleeping on an empty stomach, and having to wash my clothes at my homeboy's house.

I went to my room and counted all the money I had saved in a shoebox. I only counted it when I was home alone, because I didn't want my mom begging. I didn't mind breaking her off, but this money in the shoebox was for my dream.

I'd been spending the bare minimum from my paychecks, which were a little less than $1000 a month. I would only spend $150 a month in total, and sometimes less if I could. As soon as I got paid, I would go to the ninety-nine cents store and stock up on ramen noodles, Vienna sausages, water, cereal, and other little snacks I could find. I would go to Wal-Mart every two months and buy new shirts, sweats, boxers, socks, and toiletries for my brother and I. I loved when my mother would cook dinner occasionally though, because ramen noodles became sickening sometimes.

I counted $5000, and then put it away. I grabbed my business plan from my closet, and checked to see how much was needed to start my business, just so I could know how close I was.

"Fuck!" I shouted. I needed $15,000 more.

I closed my notebook and then said a prayer to God before getting into the shower. I needed him to bless me right now, because I felt rock bottom was just around the corner.

Once I got out, I smelled spaghetti so I knew my mom was home. Looked like tonight was one of the lucky nights that she was able to cook.

"Hey Ma," I smiled at her and tightened the towel around my waist.

"Hey Yazir," she smiled and turned the burner down.

"Did you see this?" I asked and showed her the notice.

"Mm hmm, baby sit down," she pulled a chair out.

"One second," I said and rushed off to change into some boxers, sweats, socks, and a t-shirt.

I returned to the kitchen, and a steaming plate of spaghetti was in front of the chair she'd pulled out for me. Sameer walked into the apartment just then, and sat down after speaking to us.

"Boys, I'm moving back to Mississippi to stay with my father. You guys are more than welcome to come, and he will pay for your tickets," she said and placed two cups of Kool-Aid down for us.

"Ma, Mississippi? I can't live there!" Sameer frowned.

"Me either and I ain't going," I twirled some spaghetti onto my fork.

"Then figure out what you're gonna do, because I'm leaving in three weeks and all of us have to be out by then," she exhaled and then sat down with her food.

We all ate in silence, and once I was done, I rushed to my room. I dialed my best friend Dasey, and he picked up on the third ring.

"What's up Yaz?" he answered and I could hear a girl giggling in the background.

"What's up, aye man, I need the info for your plug," I said. I ain't wanna do this shit, but I was desperate.

Dasey wasn't rich, but he stayed with knots of cash, the newest shoes and clothes, and he had a car. I wasn't interested in the material things outside of a car though. I needed this money for something greater. I was gonna invest in myself and start a business that I knew would prosper. My mother said there were certain people who achieved things at young ages, and did things way before their time, and she believed I was one of those people. I planned to be balling by my early twenties, and I was playing no games.

"Oh, now you wanna get on! I been telling you to get with this shit, man," he chuckled as some bitch kissed loudly on him.

"Whatever, just send me Vapor's info, aight?" I said.

"Sending now," he responded and I immediately hung up.

I was just gonna do this until I made enough to start my business. After that, I was getting out of the game... At least that's what I hoped.

Chapter One: Nina Joy Jeffries

Four years later...

Aubrie and I were at the mall shopping, because I needed a dress for my fiancé's event tonight. There was some sort of awards ceremony, and I needed to look good while on his arm. I really didn't want to go, because he always put so much pressure on me to be perfect. And the more I tried to be perfect, the more I fucked up. I blew out hot hair as I thought about it.

My fiancé was a guy named Seth Brooks. I met him one day when I was at the Barnes and Noble bookstore buying a mixology book. He was gorgeous as hell, and very sweet upon our initial meeting, so I was more than happy to give him my number. Over time though, he became very overbearing and critical of everything I did.

Although he was nine years older than me at thirty-two, I didn't feel like he was some creepy nigga by being interested in me. However, sometimes I did feel like he saw me as a Stepford wife, or someone he could mold into the perfect mate. It seemed as if he got with me because he felt he could turn me into whatever he wanted.

I'd just turned twenty-three a month ago, and of course, sometimes I liked to go out and wear short dresses. Seth was not a fan of me dressing my age, because he always said it was the way sluts dressed. I thought he was being over the top at first, but my mom said he was right, and that if I was gonna be with a man like him, I needed to look the part. She was very wise, so I took her advice despite my reservations.

"That looks good, Nina. Seth is gonna love that with his whack ass," my best friend Aubrie nodded her head up and down.

She hated Seth because she felt the same way I did about his criticizing and controlling ways. She didn't like that he acted more like my father than my fiancé.

Seth was in the army, and he was constantly trying to find ways to work his way up to a higher rank, which is why he needed me to be perfect tonight. I think his army background was the reason he was so strict.

Currently, he was a Staff Sargent, and because he was so hell bent on making his way up the ranks, he was always on the go, and we were always at events and shit. The parties we went to were so stuffy, and the only music being played was by a live pianist somewhere in the corner.

My mom loved Seth because he made a lot of money, was pretty established, and he loved the finer things in life. That also meant that whenever we argued, she would take his side.

"Okay, well, let's get this one," I said before going back into the dressing room.

I purchased the $80 dress, and then Aubrie and I went to brunch. Once we were finished, I went home so that I could take a nice hot bath and start to prepare for this evening. I just wanted to fast forward through it so I could come home and study my mixology book.

***

"Oh, hey honey," I said when I saw Seth walking into our bedroom. I had just gotten out of the bath, and I felt much better about tonight.

"What did you buy?" He folded his arms, getting straight to the point. I hated when he acted like this.

I tightened my robe, and then grabbed the Nordstrom's bag to retrieve the dress. It was perfect and I couldn't wait for him to see me in it.

As I stated before, Seth was a gorgeous man. He was light skinned, had gray eyes, and a muscular build. He was six feet even, and had minimal facial hair with a short fade. I was very surprised to find out he was a single man when he approached me a year back.

"I don't like it. Good thing I got you something else," he huffed and pulled a red dress out of the closet.

It was long with a split on the side, a turtleneck at the top, with long sleeves. It was a bit stuffy for my taste, and I wanted to wear the one I bought. Mine was white, mid-thigh length, and long sleeved. It hugged my slim thick body just right, but not too much. Then again, I should've known he would hate it.

"Seth that's not really my style," I responded shyly.

"This isn't a fashion show Nina, this is a very prestigious award ceremony, and I need my lady to look the part. Would Michelle Obama wear what you have in your hand?" he raised a brow. He was obsessed with Michelle Obama. What he failed to realize was that Michelle Obama was older than me.

"When she was twenty-three like me, I'm sure she would've," I chuckled but he didn't crack a smile.

"No, she wouldn't. The women that stroll Figueroa wear that. This is the dress you're wearing, Nina." He hung it on the back of the chair, just as his phone rang. I saw it was his sister Maya, and he picked it up and left to talk on it before I could even say anything.

I plopped down onto the bed, and then ran my hands over my face. Maybe I was making a big deal out of nothing. Just because he didn't like me to wear certain things, did not mean he was a bad guy. Maybe when I got older I would understand his motives, like my mother claimed she did.

I stood up to look in the mirror, and braided my long dark hair into two braids so that they could dry up and have some body waves to them. At least I had a say so in my hair for tonight.

***

"You look great, Nina." Seth walked into the room and hugged me from behind. The red did look nice against my cognac colored skin, but I still felt like an old lady. "And look, there is a split to show those sexy legs." He rubbed up my leg and then squeezed my ass, I guess attempting to make me feel better.

I half smiled and slightly moved from his embrace. I didn't feel like being groped and touched, especially by him. I put on a red headband since my hair was hanging down, and then grabbed my purse so that we could leave. He pressed his lips against mine, and because I wasn't expecting it or wanting it, it was very awkward. He grabbed my hand in his, and we headed out of the door.

The event was packed wall to wall, and all the men looked nice dressed in their uniforms. All the older women were dressed like me, and the few young women had on cute, sexy, and sophisticated dresses like the one I wanted to wear. I sighed as I took in my surroundings.

"I want you to mingle with the wives here, which means not scrolling on your phone the whole time," Seth whispered to me and I nodded. He caught me looking on my phone *once*, and he never let it go.

"Good evening ladies, this is my fiancée, Nina," Seth introduced me and they all sized me up.

None of them appeared to be my age, but I was used to that by now. I'd never met a young black girl at these events, only old white women, young Hispanic women, or old Oreo black women. I wished that I met someone I could bond with over this shit, because Aubrie would just stare at me and blink like Dora the Explorer when I complained to her about it.

"Nice to meet you ladies," I smiled and they mumbled something. Seth left me to go speak with some of the other men, so I took a seat at their table.

"So you're an army *fiancée* but not a wife I see," one lady chuckled. She looked to be about forty years old, and her fair skin was wrinkled something terrible.

"Yes, but I will be a wife soon," I giggled trying to lighten the mood. I knew she was throwing shade, but I decided to be the bigger person.

"How can you be so sure?" one other girl cocked her head. She was a Hispanic chick who appeared to be in her mid twenties. I could tell she was one of those who tried to fit in with the white women as much as she could.

"Well, I have a ring," I smiled and cleared my throat. Boy were these bitches testing me. I wanted to bend them all over and snatch the sticks out of their asses.

"Honey, a ring is just jewelry without the paperwork," an older black women chimed in and sipped her champagne.

"Paperwork is just paper," I shrugged one shoulder. I had to shoot back at these bitches just a little, because they were really trying to subtly go in on me.

"You poor thing, is that what your mama taught you?" The white lady let out a hearty laugh, and so did the others.

"Let's not speak on my mother. But one thing she did teach me was to show respect and to be classy, which I can see your mother failed to show you," I spat and they gasped.

They looked at each other as if I'd just said the unthinkable. I immediately regretted it once I remembered where I was at, and how important it was.

"Well, I'm gonna tell you something that your mother definitely doesn't know, and that's to let Seth know that he can kiss that promotion goodbye. My husband wouldn't dare give him a promotion while he's with someone like you," the white lady raised a brow. She must've been the General's wife, fuck!

"No wait, I-" The three of them got up from the table, and ignored me as I tried to stop them. A couple minutes later, Seth sat down at the table with me and kissed my face.

"Where are the ladies?" he inquired.

"They umm, they went to mingle," I lied. He was gonna fucking kill me if that lady meant anything of what she'd said to me.

"You should've went along too. Nina, don't mess this up for me," he gritted.

"Fine," I stood up quickly, a little too quickly, and his drink spilled onto my lap.

"Nina, what the fuck! That is an $800 dress girl!" He barked at me as I tried to clean the Brandy off my lap. A few people looked over, and I was embarrassed at my actions, and at the way he scolded me like a child.

"I'm sorry, Seth, I-"

"Let's go!" He yanked my arm and pulled me towards the exit. Please Lord, if this is a nightmare wake me up.

"Seth, you're hurting me, stop it!" I tried to release my arm from him but it didn't work.

Once we got to his car, he opened the door to his Infiniti, and threw me in like I weighed nothing. I put my feet into the car, and then closed my door. He got in on the driver's side, and slammed his door so hard I thought the glass was gonna break.

"Are you crazy, Seth! It wasn't that serious! My arm is killing-"

WHAM!

My face hit the window, and blood spilled from my nose immediately after. I touched it gently in disbelief, and then stared at the blood on my fingertips for a couple moments, as I listened to him pant like the Incredible Hulk. Tears began to spill from my eyes as I looked at the blood. Funny enough, I was crying because I was so unhappy, not because I just got my nose busted. Seth had never hit me, but being with him was a miserable experience all on it's own. This was just the cherry on top.

"I'm gonna find a ride," I whispered and reached for the door lever. My nose was still dripping, but all I cared about was getting away from him.

"Nina, I'm sorry baby. I am just very upset with you right now. You know how important this is to me, and you're acting like you don't know what to do!" He banged on the steering wheel. His tone went from calm to enraged in a matter of seconds, just like a rollercoaster before the drop.

I stared out the front windshield and let the tears race down my cheeks. I didn't care to stop them or the blood. I was still holding onto the lever, so I pulled it and exited the car without another word. I started to walk, and I heard Seth crank the car up and follow me.

"Nina, get back in the car before my colleagues see your face!" Seth gritted.

I ignored him and pulled my phone out to dial my friend Madison for a ride. Aubrie was working the night shift at Dream Bar and Cafe, so I knew she couldn't get me. Plus, I didn't want Aubrie trying to fuck Seth up tonight.

As I spoke with Madison so she could pick me up, Seth called me all kinds of stupid bitches and dumb hoes. The way he belittled me made more tears come out of my eyes. The cry was silent with the exception of a few sniffles, but it hurt just as much as a loud one did.

"Nina, if you don't get back in the car I'm done with you!" he screamed, using every muscle in his body.

I refused to acknowledge him, so he pulled off, getting smoke in my face. I waved it and coughed before plopping down on the sidewalk to wait for Madison. I was over this! I was over him!

About twenty minutes later, she pulled up in her Civic, and leaned over to open the passenger door while still in the driver seat.

"Damn bitch, what happened?" she quizzed once I got in.

"Seth happened," I sniffled, and winced due to the pain in my nose.

"Giirrrl," she smacked her lips and then turned up the radio. Madison knew I didn't want to talk about it, and unlike Aubrie, she would never try and force it out of me.

She picked up her speed and then took me to a hotel to sleep. I didn't want to go to my mother's house, because I didn't feel like hearing her take Seth's side. My only home was with Seth, and I definitely wasn't going there.

I handed Madison $20 which she denied, and then climbed out to book a room at the Hyatt House in El Segundo.

Once I was all set, I took a long hot bath, and then cried myself to sleep. As weird as it may sound, I prayed for this to be the end of Seth and I.

Chapter One: Yazir Willis

"Oooh baby, shit," my long time fuck buddy, Gabriella called out as I plunged in and out of her from the back.

The sight of her big round ass bouncing and jiggling everywhere was the greatest shit ever. I could watch that shit all day if it wasn't attached to that annoying ass mouth and stuck up ass attitude.

"Uuhh," she cried out as I smacked and squeezed her ass. I gripped her hair in my hands, and went ham before pulling out and filling the condom up.

"Shit, Gabi," I panted as I slowly pulled the condom off of my dick.

I didn't wanna spill a drop on my Egyptian Cotton, nor did I want her to scoop it up and save it. I know it sounds far fetched, but a bitch like Gabriella could find a way out of no fucking way.

"Why do you always pull out even though you're wearing a condom?" she quizzed with a frown. See what I meant? Why did it fucking matter?

"Because I don't want no fucking kids," I responded and grabbed my blunt from the ashtray next to me.

"You don't want kids period? Or you just don't want them with me?" she raised her thin brow.

Why ask questions that she knew she didn't want the answer to? It's not like I was the type of nigga to sugarcoat, or do anything to preserve someone's feelings; especially those of a bitch that I only stuck my dick in.

"I don't want them with *you* or any other bitch," I replied honestly as I took a pull.

"Why?" she questioned further.

"Because I don't love you and I never could, even if you did have my baby. I wanna love my child's mother, or at least have love *for* her, and you and I will never have that," I stared into her eyes intensely, and she stared back into mine. Her lip trembled a little bit, which made me exhale heavily. "You better stop with that crying shit," I shook my head and took another toke of the blunt. She promptly looked away, I guess to get her face together, and then turned back to look at me.

Gabriella was a cool chick but she was way too thirsty and ready. She gave way too much to a nigga who cared nothing about her like that. A woman that would be willing to act like my wife before I even told her I loved her, or took her out on a date wasn't my type. I wanted a woman who would demand respect from me, and make me work for what I wanted. With Gabriella, the pussy and the benefits came too fucking easy. She would do anything for me, and she wasn't even close to being my girlfriend. It's not like she thought she was either, she knew what was up. Her eagerness to please me, no matter how I treated her was a major turn off. What did my mom used to say to my girl cousins? Oh, never play girlfriend to a friend, and never play wife to a boyfriend. That shit was true, and Gabriella needed to learn that.

"Ain't nobody crying Yaz, but I think a baby would be good for you," she chuckled to herself. I knew it was a nervous laugh due to her saying such a dumb ass thing. She had to say anything to save face from almost crying just a minute ago.

"I'm twenty-one years old and I ain't trying to be nobody's daddy, husband, boyfriend, or nothing," I scoffed and then stood up. "You need to get dressed if you walking in with me at my party tonight," I told her and then grabbed some towels from my towel warmer. I was done with the dumb shit; I had a celebration to get to.

"You know I'm walking in with you. I just wished Kiara didn't have to walk in with you too," she rolled her eyes and turned her lip up before getting out of the bed.

"Sharing is caring," I said before heading into my bathroom. I had plenty of dick, and there was no need to be stingy.

I walked into the bathroom, and looked in the mirror. I was young, black, and rich, and it wasn't shit a nigga or bitch could say to me. I struggled the majority of my twenty-one years, until I finally was able to start my own business at age nineteen. Now, I was the owner and creator of Blue Dream rolling papers and Dream Bar and Club.

Like I said, I wasn't a nigga who was born into money whatsoever. I worked hard as hell for everything that I have today. I worked every job you can think of from mowing lawns, to being a gas station attendant, to being a mover, all the way to a corner boy. Sometimes I worked three jobs at once if that's what it took for me to get my business off the ground. I didn't mind sacrificing having fun and shit, because I knew it would soon be worth it. 'Work hard now, play hard later' was my motto for years.

After pushing weight for about ten months, I was able to get a patent for *my* specific type of flavored blunt papers. A few more thousands later, I was able to get them mass-produced to sell out of my trunk. I would be selling bags of cocaine, pills, weed, and my blunt papers all fucking day and night, and didn't care how much sleep I lost. Thanks to word of mouth, my blunt papers became the shit to have, and I was offered a distribution deal to some major liquor stores. Two years later, here I am today and boy am I proud.

Everyone knew me as the young nigga who made it out the hood with his own company. Niggas around me were too focused on impressing the bitches around them with a few bands or so, but not I. I didn't give a fuck about these hoes. I had no problem with women whether I was balling out of control or on the corner begging, so there was no need for me to floss for them. Instead, I saved my shit for a greater cause, and still got plenty of pussy along the way, without dropping a damn dime.

Outside of being a business owner, some also knew me as the king of the streets of Los Angeles. Yeah, you guessed it, I push weight still. I started from selling bags on the corners and cooking in the trap, to now being the nigga that muthafuckas reported to. I used to work for this dude named Vapor, and because I was so dedicated to the cause, when he got lung cancer and died, it was only right that I took over.

Niggas already bowed down when they saw me anyway, so the shift was beyond natural.

I was a nigga who paid attention to detail, whether it was how many diamonds were in my cufflinks, or how many muthafuckas that bought from each trap I had set up, I always kept up. Anything that had my name on it was being watched very closely, but I was big enough to have people doing the little shit for me too. Some stuff was just a complete waste of a boss nigga's time.

If you worked for me and had to see me, it was never a good thing. You know those managers that only come out when you're getting fired or some shit? That was me.

On the contrary, every nigga I put on has met with me so I could feel them out initially, but after that, we should never have to speak. I don't just put any nigga looking to make a quick buck on my team either. And I may not be in your face twenty-four seven, but I know who you are and what you add to my operation. I found it funny when niggas thought they were too low on the ladder for me to catch them slipping. You should see how their eyes damn near pop out of their heads when I pull up on their asses.

From Blue Dream, to my bar, and to being a kingpin, I was living large and oh so well. Flashy wasn't my style, but you could smell the money on me. I didn't look like drug money either; I looked and smelled like old money.

My partners in crime were my older brother Sameer and my best friend Dasey. We'd been to hell and back together as far as the drug game, so it felt good to be able to enjoy the fruits of our labor. We've been shot at, robbed, jumped, you name it, it has happened. But we all prospered and that's all that mattered.

Once out the shower, I sprayed a few spritz of my cologne while I was still wet. I looked up to see Gabriella watching me with a lustful smile. I gave her smirk, and then walked up on her. She scooted to the edge of the bed, titties still out, and began to loosen my towel from around my waist. She picked up my ten inches, and began to suck on the tip like it contained medicine she needed. I let her go for a little while, and then I pulled back.

"I told you to get ready," I spat and then turned around so I could get dressed. I looked over my shoulder at her, and she hopped up to do as I had asked.

Once dressed, I stood in the mirror and admired my look from head to toe. Everything on my body was Versace, right down to my socks. I had a few iced out pieces on my neck and wrists, but not too much, because a lot of jewelry really wasn't my thing.

Gabriella had on an orange number, and her body was looking right in it. I grabbed her ass roughly, and bit my lip as I imagined it in it's bare state. She chuckled a bit, and then I opened my bedroom door for her to walk out. When we got outside, there was my driver in a black, Platinum version, bulletproof Escalade. He opened the back door for Gabriella and I, and then went around so he could take us to Kiara.

***

"Hey Yaz," Kiara smiled as she climbed into the truck with Gabriella and I.

I kissed her on her neck, and gripped her smooth thigh. Kiara was sexy as hell from her smooth caramel complexion, to her slanted honey eyes. Kiara was the perfect fuck buddy because she gave me the pussy whenever I wanted, and didn't nag me afterward. On top of that, she was freaky as fuck, just how I liked them. Gabriella had a nice golden complexion, long blonde hair or weave, whatever the fuck it was, and a body that would make you wanna go to church every day and sometimes twice on Sunday. Physically she was a banger but mentally, nah.

Kiara and Gabriella used to be best friends, but they let this good dick get in between them; mainly Gabriella. It all started with a couple freaky ass threesomes, and then they began to bicker because Gabriella felt I was fucking Kiara longer. Neither one of them were even close to being someone I would take down to meet my moms in Mississippi, but I didn't wanna waste my energy telling them that. I don't think Kiara would even care, but I didn't wanna find out.

Gabriella and I always had threesomes with different chicks, and that's the only reason I fucked with her like that, even though she had a trashy personality. Outside of the bedroom, she was annoying, stuck up, too damn available, and a gold digger. Funny thing is, I've never bought her ass shit because I didn't believe in spending money on a woman I didn't love. I think she hoped that one day I would, and a part of me knew she had accidentally fallen in love with my young ass, no matter how hard she pretended she was just having fun like me. She was twenty-seven, six years older than me by the way.

I caressed Kiara's exposed thigh again, because they were thick as fuck, and chuckled when I saw Gabriella scoff. She was staring out the window now, I guess because she was angry. I laughed to myself at her behavior.

We arrived to Dream Bar and my driver came around to open the door. People were talking and being loud, but not loud enough to drown out the music coming from inside the club. We were led to the VIP area where I spotted my brother, best friend, and my cousin Matthew. I made a mental reminder to get at Matthew about some business shit tomorrow morning.

“What's up, y'all?” I grinned and dapped them all up. I was excited. It always felt good to party after accomplishing a task.

Tonight was to celebrate the release of a new line of blunt papers, and ultimately new and more money coming my way. I planned to get drunk as fuck tonight, and then end the night with Gabriella, Kiara, and hopefully something new too. Yeah, I was on my frisky as fuck tip.

As I bobbed my head to the music, munched on some Skittles, and watched Gabriella twerk her fat ass in my lap, a waitress came up with a bucket of alcohol, juices, cups, and ice.

“Here you are,” she said and set it on the glass table in front of us.

When she picked her head up, I was at a loss for words. This was the prettiest fucking girl I had ever seen in my twenty-one years. She had smooth skin the color of my favorite drink, Hennessy X.O., long dark hair, I'm talking to her tailbone, and a banging ass body.

“Can I get you guys anything else?” she asked and looked around at all of us.

She had a little nose piercing, perfect full lips, and deep brown eyes. She wore a tank top that read Dream Bar and exposed her flat stomach, and shorts that fit just right. Even though she had very little on, I knew she was a classy one.

I slowly moved Gabriella out of my lap as we made eye contact again. “Hi, I'm the owner, Yazir Willis. I can't believe I've never seen you before,” I towered over her.

“What the fuck!” I heard Gabriella yelp.

“Oh wow, nice to meet you. I'm Nina,” she half smiled and stuck her hand out to me. She probably thought I was some creep from the way I was looking down at her.

“That's a sexy ass name,” I bit my lip and she chuckled.

“Thank you, Mr. Willis. Well, if you guys need anything, just press the blue button. I will be over at the bar,” she said and started off.

I waited for her to turn around so I could look down at her ass, and it was perfectly round. It wasn't as big as Gabriella's, but it would definitely do. The backs of her thighs were so smooth, causing me to lick my lips. I couldn't help myself so I followed after her.

“Excuse me Nina, are you seeing anybody, beautiful?” I smiled down at her. I didn't give a fuck about Gabriella, Kiara, or any other jump off I may have fucked up in here.

“What's it to you?” she folded her arms.

"I wanted to get your number or something," I smirked.

"Didn't you just have a girl in your lap? Isn't that your girlfriend?" She cocked her head.

"What? Hell no. But forget about that, can I get your number?" I questioned again. Damn, I had never had to work this hard for a number... ever. I usually didn't even have to say much, if anything at all.

"I think you're too young for me, and secondly, I have a fiancé," she showed me her ring.

"How old are you?" I quizzed. She looked to be about twenty-one like me. Her fiancé was the least of my fucking worries.

"I'm twenty-three," she rolled her neck. Attitude, I liked that shit. I knew right then that the pussy was good.

"What's two years?" I grabbed her small waist and she tensed up a little.

She fit perfectly into my big hands, and I just imagined lifting her up and sliding her down onto my dick. Her skin was supple, just like I had imagined, and her perfume was soft but very prevalent.

We stared at each other in silence, as "Back to Sleep" by Chris Brown played, and a smile spread across her pretty face. Her smile could turn heads alone, even under the dim light of the club.

"Hey Yaz," some random pushed up on me.

Nina shook her head at me with a laugh, and then moved my hands off her body. She rushed through the crowd and disappeared before I could go after her.

"Shit," I grumbled and lightly bumped the thirsty chick that ruined my game.

"For real? Was she that cute, Yaz?" Gabriella folded her arms across her breasts once I sat back down in VIP.

"Shut up." I turned my lip up and shook my head, before pulling Kiara into my lap.

Nina had another thing coming if she thought she'd gotten rid of me that easily. I've been told that when I met the woman I was gonna marry, I would know it, and I think I just met her.

Chapter Two: Nina Joy

I walked over to the bar I was working from, and when I got there, Aubrie and Madison were smiling.

“What the fuck?” I chuckled at their asses.

Madison was a dancer here. She was supposed to be in her cage dancing to the music, but she was always just hanging at the bar.

“I saw you got Yazir Willis' attention,” Aubrie grinned and so did Madison.

“So what,” I shrugged and started to fill another bucket with ice.

I can't lie, I was definitely intrigued by him, and I was for sure feeling myself now that I had caught his attention.

“Girl, he followed you all the way down here!” Madison shouted and smiled.

“I'm sure he's just trying to get me in bed like all these other hoes. Also, let's not forget that I am getting married ladies,” I exhaled.

“To a nigga who wants to be your damn daddy,” Madison spat and folded her arms. She didn't care for Seth either, but no one hated him as much as Aubrie did.

“I thought you broke up with him Nina. And you never told me why by the way,” Aubrie said as she prepared a drink for a patron.

“Because it's nothing really,” I replied and gave Madison a look so that she wouldn't say anything.

"Whatever, so are y'all back together? Because if not, you should definitely look into Yazir." Aubrie ran her tongue over her teeth. "His brother and homeboy are pretty cute too, from what I can see," she added.

"Yazir is way too young Brie, come on now," I huffed and chuckled, purposely ignoring her question regarding Seth.

Yazir looked twenty-five, but when you first get hired here you have to learn all about his sexy ass.

"What is he, twenty-two?" Madison placed her hand on her hip, and sipped her drink with the other hand.

"Worse, twenty-one. I like grown men like Seth," I half lied.

I liked grown men, but I wasn't sure how much I liked Seth at this point. I felt like I was living my life for my mother and not myself. Marrying Seth would make my mother the happiest woman on Earth, and that always made me happy in return.

Ever since I got pregnant at age sixteen, I've been working my ass off to make my mother proud of me again. That's why I was going hard at this bartending thing, because I hoped to be a world-renowned bartender one day. I wanted to make something of myself.

Seth didn't care too much for my career choice, but that was one thing I couldn't let him dictate in my life. I loved the art of drink making, and no man could take that from me. It seemed that Seth didn't like anything I did. I wondered why he was even with me. The only time we agreed on anything was when I was on my back.

"Twenty-one, shmenity-one. That nigga is fine, paid, and I'm sure the dick is phenomenal," Aubrie responded. "I've heard rumors," she whispered and cackled. I shook my head at her and then pulled some bottles from the cooler.

I walked the bucket to the VIP area next to Yazir's. I looked out the corner of my eye, and he and the chick that was in his lap initially were watching me. He now had a new bitch in his lap, but she was too busy popping her ass to notice where his attention was. He flashed his beautiful smile before popping a Skittle into his mouth, and my juices started to flow. I could already feel how well he could sex me. You know those dudes that just look like they can fuck? That was Yazir. From his commanding demeanor to his cocky tone, it all screamed *I can have you climbing the walls.*

Yazir was fine as fuck, and nothing about him said little boy besides his age. He was 6'4, had a deep caramel complexion, a beard, and perfectly tapered yet unkempt hair. He was muscular, and his cologne was something I would trade oxygen for. And the way his hands felt when he grabbed my waist, it was all too much.

"Damn," I whispered to myself as I thought about him.

"Excuse me, hello!" some guy snapped in my face.

"Oh, I'm sorry," I half smiled.

"I only forgive you because you're sexy as hell," the guy licked his crusty lips. You could tell he was out spending some money he didn't have, but hey, I was no one's accountant.

"I appreciate that," I responded dryly.

"Let me get some wings and your number on the side," he grinned.

"I'm married, and your wings will be on their way soon," I sighed and rushed off before he could say anything else.

I put the guys order in, and then almost jumped for joy when I saw it was time for me to go home. This was the first night in a long time that I was not getting off at three fucking a.m. I would actually be able to catch up on some shows I had in my Netflix list, without falling asleep ten minutes in.

I waited to deliver the guy's food, and then I went to check on Yazir's table so I could take any empty glasses, new orders, and let them know I was leaving.

"Is there anything else I can get you guys before I clock out?" I quizzed. I made sure to give Yazir plenty eye contact. He was nibbling on some chick's ear.

"We're good, beautiful," he glanced over at me and then resumed what he was doing.

"Okay, have a goodnight," I sighed and then turned to leave with the empty glasses I'd collected.

I dropped them off in the kitchen, and then headed to the locker room. As I was walking, I looked up into Yazir's section, and he and his friends were going in as something by Young Thug played. I just smiled at how much fun they were having, and then went to clock out.

The hotel I was staying at started to get expensive, so I was back home with my mom now. I hated to be there, because all she wanted to talk about was Seth this and Seth that, and how I should go home to him. This was a way out for me, but I wasn't quite sure if that was what I wanted. I was never one to make hasty decisions.

"Seth called again, and he sent these," my mother pointed to three gift boxes.

"I don't wanna talk to him right now," I huffed and plopped down on the couch. I'd just walked in the door, and she had already started.

"Baby, what happened between you two?" She asked and sat next to me.

I stared up at the ceiling, contemplating if I wanted to tell her the truth or not. I decided to go ahead and be honest, so that maybe she would agree with me on leaving Seth. I had initially kept the reasoning from her, because I didn't want her to go crazy on Seth, but now I think it would work to my advantage.

"Mom, he hit me," I sat up and looked at her. She stared at me, and then rubbed my hair back.

"He's sorry baby, can't you see?" she kissed my cheek and I was dumbfounded by her answer.

"My nose was busted Ma, and he-"

"And he didn't mean it, Nina. He sent you gifts and he came by begging me to talk to you," she cut me off.

"But Mom, isn't that why you left my father?" I frowned in confusion. I was floored right now.

"Honey, your father wasn't worth the shit stains in his drawers. Seth is a good man, and he loves you. Sometimes you have to endure the pain to be by the side of a good man, baby. Don't let that run you off and allow some other skank to get your spot," she half smiled.

"But Ma-".

"Nina, just give him another chance. You guys love each other," she stood up and kissed my forehead. Did I love him? Or did I love the idea of being in love with someone?

I watched her switch off into her room, and then snatched up my belongings off the couch. I went to put my phone on the charger, and then pinned my hair up to wash my face so that I could inspect my nose. It was finally healing up, and I wouldn't have to wear as much make up anymore. I stared in the mirror for a little bit, as my mother's words circled my mind.

I didn't know what to do, and I was so confused. I always looked to my mother for her advice, but at this point I wasn't so sure. I was really trying to build a life with Seth, but the more I tried, the unhappier I felt. Did I really wanna spend the rest of my life with this man? I knew I didn't but how could I tell my mother that? And what if I was wrong about what was good for me?

I took a long hot bath, with bubbles and everything, and then slipped on my short nightgown. I climbed in bed, and then took my phone off the charger. I saw a text from Aubrie, and then one from an unknown number.

Aubrie: *I gave him your number!*

Me: *Who?*

I sat up in my bed, but kept my lamp off.

Aubrie: *Yazir bitch. Lol. I took over their table and his brother was on me. As we were exchanging info, Yazir asked me what was up with you.*

Me: *I hate you!*

I texted back. For some reason I was excited about this little ass boy having my number.

Aubrie: *Bitch I just changed your life! You're gonna owe me when you fall in love!*

I backed out of our conversation, and then clicked the unknown number.

+1 (323) 555- 9862: *Lock me in beautiful. You know who this is.*

I rolled my eyes and locked my phone. A small smile covered my face, and then I drifted off to sleep.

Chapter Two: Aubrie Gibson

An hour earlier...

"Is everybody doing okay up here?" I asked the VIP section I was just assigned.

"I was doing okay, but now I'm doing better," I heard a deep voice call out.

I looked to my right, and I saw the sexiest chocolate nigga ever. He had dreads that were long as hell, and big brown eyes. Even though he was sitting down, I could tell that he was about 6'4. He was sitting next to Yazir, the club's owner, and they looked a lot alike so I knew they were related. They both had beards and perfect full lips, except Yazir was a dark caramel.

"Oh yeah, and why is that?" I quizzed while biting my lip. I was never the type of bitch to front, and I could see in his eyes that he wanted to fuck me as bad as I wanted to fuck him.

"Because you're up here. Come closer so I won't have to talk so loud." He waved me over and I got a whiff of his cologne when he did so. I switched over there, and Yazir was smiling with his cute ass, as the festivities went on.

"What's up?" I folded my arms and poked my hip out.

I was no Halle Berry, but if you couldn't have her, me or my best friends Nina and Madison were next in line. I had smooth light skin, hazel eyes, and I kept a long weave in my head that touched the middle of my back. I was the type of girl who kept her hair and nails done always. You would never catch Madison, Nina, or me with a fucked up pedicure or manicure.

"What's up with you? What's your name?" he quizzed.

"It's Aubrie, but some people just call me Brie," I chuckled and he nodded with a grin.

"Oh word? That's pretty, and it fits. My name is Sameer, this is my brother Yazir, and his best friend Dasey," he introduced me, and I shook all of their hands.

Dasey was cute as hell, too. He was light skinned like me, and was rocking a fade and diamond grills.

"Nice to meet you, fellas," I said as I shook all their hands. I liked that none of them had rough ashy hands, or dirty fingernails. I always checked because that was a big turn off for me.

"So let me get your digits, Aubrie." Sameer looked up at me and I got chills. Damn, I was light but I loved me some chocolate, especially when they were muscular and tall like Sameer.

"Okay," I smiled and read off my number to him.

"And what's up with your pretty ass friend? She dissed me hard," his brother Yazir asked me. His eyes were squinted, and I could tell he really wanted to figure Nina out.

I was never team Seth, so I would be happy to help Yazir bag my friend. She needed someone she could be herself with, and have fun with too. Nina was very colorful, and she was a blast to hang out with, but when daddy Seth came around, she was like a child on punishment.

"I can give you her number and you can see what's up with her yourself," I offered with the raise of a brow.

"Shit, even better. It's good to know you're willing to help your friend out. She don't know what she's missing by dissing a nigga like myself," he grinned and placed his hand over his chest.

"Don't be so modest," I said sarcastically and he chuckled.

He handed me his phone, and I typed Nina's number in as some chick stared me down with eyes full of hate. I'm guessing she was Yazir's little freak of the week or something, but if she didn't have the balls to check him, that wasn't my problem.

"There you go," I handed Yazir his phone back and he nodded.

The chick shot daggers at me, hopped up off the velvet couch, and stormed out of the VIP area. Yazir didn't flinch or anything, showing that he didn't care about her at all. He didn't even look in the direction she walked off in, but it was obvious that he knew she had gotten up angrily. Damn, that shit must hurt.

"But anyway beautiful, I'm gon' call you," Sameer snapped me from my thoughts of old girl.

"You better," I winked and turned on my heels.

As I walked off, I pretended to be looking at something to my right, but I was looking to see if Sameer was watching my ass. I smirked when I saw him watching, as I made my way to and down the steps of the VIP area.

"I see you decided to get at Yazir yourself," Madison said, still sitting at the bar.

"Actually bitch, I was helping myself to his fine ass brother Sameer," I bucked my eyes at her nosey ass. "And ain't you supposed to be up there dancing or some shit. You don't get paid to sip drinks at the bar, Madison," I shook my head and then started preparing the drinks on the receipts that were lined up.

"I get paid to look bomb as fuck and do what the fuck I wanna do," she cocked her head, and sipped her Midori Sour. Just then, the manager walked up and tapped Madison on the shoulder.

"The owner is in the house and you have the nerve to be down here taking forty-five minute breaks?" he fumed.

"I didn't-"

"Get in your cage now before I dock your pay, Madison!" He cut in and yanked her off the stool as I died laughing. *That's what her lazy ass gets,* I thought to myself.

The rest of the night I was on cloud nine, because I was getting paid to flirt with a fine ass nigga, and I had possibly found my best friend a new love interest.

Chapter Two: Yazir

I woke up early as fuck with Gabriella and Kiara on each side of me. No matter how much they bickered, they always put that shit to the side after a few drinks and some dick.

I looked at the clock, which read 8am, and then gathered what I needed to get ready for the day. I set up everything in the bathroom, and then went to the laundry room to speak with my housekeeper Brenda.

"Good morning, Ms. Brenda, please escort the ladies out when I leave. Don't allow any showers or anything, and I will leave money for a cab or an Uber," I smiled and she shook her head.

I didn't want them in my house while I wasn't there, so showering and eating breakfast and shit was not an option at the moment.

"Fine Yazir, but you are a mess," she snickered and folded the towels. I laughed and then rushed back upstairs to shower.

I was ready to go by 9:45am, and then hopped into my G-Wagon. I checked my phone and saw that sexy Nina had yet to respond to my text message. I chuckled to myself and shook my head. If she wanted to play hard to get that was fine with me, but she was gonna be mine either way. What Nina didn't know, was that I worked hard for what I wanted and I always got it. Right now, my eyes were set on her, regardless of whether she was actually engaged or not. If he really loved her, he would let her go be with a nigga who was more befitting for her. I laughed to myself at my own thoughts, because I knew that was bullshit. Nigga had no choice though. I was coming for his lady and I was leaving with her.

I was headed to one of my smoke shops on Crenshaw, just a little past Rosecrans in the Hawthorne area. This wasn't quite the hood, but you still didn't wanna be out over here too late at night. My older cousin Matthew managed this shop, and I wanted to make sure he was providing the quality of service that I expected. I didn't care that he was my family; if you weren't working and performing to my standards, you had to go.

Lately, this particular smoke shop hadn't been selling as much, and when I checked on Yelp, there were complaints that people had to wait ten to fifteen minutes before someone even came out to assist them. A part of me knew Matthew was a borderline fuck up, which is why I put him in this location, but I wanted all of my shops to provide a positive and professional experience regardless of the area.

I wanted everybody and their mama coming to buy my brand of blunt papers. I even wanted the muthafuckas who didn't smoke interested in my shit. And if I needed to cancel out the somewhat nepotism I was practicing, then so be it.

I parked in front of the Thai restaurant located next door, and then walked inside. Just like the reviews said, no one was out front, but the shop looked pristine at least. I made it to the counter, and banged on the bell repeatedly. Finally, some bitch emerged wearing little ass shorts and a tube top. She had long ass dookie braids, long curved fingernails, with blue eye shadow and the lipstick to match.

"Oh shit," she mumbled and then rushed to the back, booty cheeks jiggling and everything. I was hot as fuck by this point, because I had no idea who this bitch was, and he had her in my shop. On top of that, her attire was extremely inappropriate.

I leaned on the counter and waited until Matthew's under performing ass appeared.

"Cuz, what's up?" He smiled and put his hand out to slap mine. I roughly moved his shit out the way, and he adjusted his hat in embarrassment.

"Who the fuck is that bitch you got up in here? And why aren't you out here ready to work!" I barked and then booked it to the back.

Matthew was on my heels as I made it to the office he had. We passed that hood rat, and she was nibbling on her long ass nail like she was frightened or some shit.

"I was just using the bathroom," he said.

"You lying like fuck, Matthew! I've been reading reviews about how bad customer service is here! Why is it that this is the only location not bringing in as much as every other store?" I squinted my eyes and put my hands in my pants pockets.

"Man, them muthafuckas is lying. I be out there assisting everybody," he shrugged.

"Matthew, you got one fucking week to improve. If this week's sales don't skyrocket even a smidgen, you're gonna be looking in the wanted ads," I threatened.

"For real? Your own fucking cousin?" He shook his head.

Matthew was from Mississippi like the rest of my family, and he came down here to live a couple years ago. My aunt asked me to keep an eye on him, but shit, he was older than me at twenty-four. I tried to help him by giving him this position, even though I knew I shouldn't have. But he begged and begged, and swore up and down that he would do a good job. I should've went with my first mind, and had him answering phones or some shit.

"Yes, my own fucking cousin. Nobody comes before my fucking bread and you know that. And you're being disrespectful as fuck by having that hoe up in my shit. She better not be getting paid either," I stood up. He shook his head at me and scoffed.

"I knew once you got rich as fuck you was gon' change," he smacked his lips.

"Ain't nothing wrong with change my nigga, and that's what you fail to realize. You're twenty-four years old and haven't made any moves to better your life. You moved down here to fuck on Instagram bitches that you felt you couldn't get down South! You got four kids back in Mississippi, and how long you gonna keep feeding them that bullshit about flying them out when you get on your feet, huh?" I scowled down at him.

"Man, don't worry about my fucking kids, aight?" He twisted up his mouth, I guess embarrassed in front of his little bitch.

"Nah, I am, because I'm the one sending your baby mama money every month so they can eat and shit. Get that shit together my nigga, or you can take your ass back down to Greenville," I gritted and then left the shop.

After tearing into Matthew, I went to get some Woody's Barbecue with my best friend Dasey. He was like a brother from another mother, and he knew a lot about how weak Matthew was.

"I hate that this fucking place is so crowded, but it's good as hell," Dasey frowned as he bit into his rib tip.

"Tell me about it. I don't know what they put in this fucking sauce, but it's bomb as fuck," I commented. "Still ain't better than Peanut Red's down in Mississippi though," I added.

"Nigga, stop bringing them up. I have yet to try them, and it pisses me off whenever you bring them up. We need to go down there soon though," he said.

"Yeah, maybe for the summer or some shit," I responded.

"So what happened with Matt? Last I checked you said he was backsliding with the shop?" Dasey questioned.

"I paid him a visit today, and just like the reviews said, he was in the back fucking around," I sighed and Dasey shook his head. "But get this, I ring the bell, and out walks some Alabama porch monkey bitch in a too tight top and booty shorts," I bucked my eyes and he burst into laughter.

"Where the fuck she come from?" he grinned.

"Nigga, you tell me, shit. She reminded me of Joi from Friday, but the busted can of biscuits version." I shook my head as he chuckled.

"I thought this nigga had a bitch and like six kids," he frowned.

"Yeah, he has a girl named Robyn, and four kids. I don't know what this nigga is doing man, but he ain't about to be bullshitting on my fucking dime."

It was Sunday, and if by Saturday night the sales weren't up to par, Matthew was gonna be out on his ass. Blood or not.

Chapter Three: Nina Joy

I sat outside Seth's place, inside my car. I'd been here for at least twenty minutes, contemplating if this is where I in fact wanted to be. A little bit of me wondered if my mom was right about Seth. This was the first time he hit me, and if he was really sorry then it was worth a shot, I guess. I was currently having a problem differentiating my love for the idea of love versus my love for Seth, if there was any.

I got out of the car and smoothed down my dress. It was a simple black dress that stopped a little bit above my knees. I knew Seth would hate it but I didn't care. My long hair was in a simple ponytail, because I didn't care to dress up too much for him. I walked slowly up to Seth's door, and paused for a few moments before ringing the doorbell.

"Beautiful, I missed you. Come in," he grinned and moved back so that I could walk in.

He had some Ginuwine playing softly in the background, and a couple unscented candles burning. I walked over to his couch, and then sat down.

"So, what made you finally come home to me?" He sat next to me and rubbed my leg.

"I guess I believed you were sorry," I shrugged and fidgeted with my purse strap.

"I'm glad you believe me, Nina, because I am. I love you more than anything and I never wanted to hurt you," he caressed my face and then gently kissed my lips.

Our lips parted, and he slid his tongue into my mouth. Seth was a great kisser, and I loved when we kissed. He ran his hand under my dress, and pulled on my underwear before spreading my legs. He dropped down to his knees, and tugged my panties past my sandals before removing them. He pushed my legs further apart, lifted my dress over my butt, and then began to feast on my center.

"Mm, baby," I whispered as he made love to me with his mouth. I caressed the back of his head, and he squeezed my ass gently. "Fuck, I love you, Seth," I whimpered. I always loved him when he ate my pussy, but those feelings faded once I came.

I wound my hips onto his face, and he lapped up all my juices like a good doggy. Once I exploded, he stood up and pulled my dress over my head. He carried me to the bedroom, and then laid me down. He removed all of his clothes, and I admired his chiseled body.

My mind then drifted to what Yazir's body looked like under that suit he wore to Dream Bar. He'd texted me a couple times, but I had yet to respond. He wasn't my type, and hopefully he would one day get the picture. To be honest, I didn't want him to be my type, and I was scared that he just might be my perfect match. I wasn't one of those girls that enjoyed being with a guy that every girl wanted. I would be perfectly fine being the only chick interested in my man. With Yazir, he was extremely sought after, which was a turn off, but at the same time sexy as hell.

I closed my eyes to rid my mind of Yazir, and by the time I opened them, Seth was kissing my thighs, and then climbing between them.

"I love you, Nina," he cooed and I just gave him a half smile.

He tried to enter me raw, but I placed my hand on his pelvis and shook my head. He paused, smacked his lips, and then grabbed and rolled a condom down, before placing the head of his dick at my opening. Seth was a good seven inches, but he knew how to work it.

"Uhhh," I purred in his ear as he worked himself in and out of me.

He cupped one of my breasts, and then flicked his tongue over my nipple as he pounded my center gently. I felt myself about to cum, just as he started to jack rabbit me. A couple pumps later he was filling up the condom, and I tried to force my orgasm to hurry up. Unfortunately, his dick was limp by the time I came, and the orgasm was underwhelming. He panted heavily and started to kiss on my neck, but all I could think about was taking a shower.

Sex with Seth was a hit or miss. Sometimes I came nice and hard, and sometimes I came too late or not at all. One thing I did notice was that I always felt like I was fucking a random person. I didn't feel any connection when we made love. It was nothing like with my ex-boyfriend Phillip. I may have been sixteen, but I could feel the love between us when we had sex. With Seth, it was so empty; almost like a prostitute with one of her johns.

He finally rolled off of me after placing about one thousand kisses on my neck and shoulder, and disgusting me in the process. I sat up, and then looked over my shoulder at him slowly dozing off, with the condom still on his now shriveled dick. I pretended to throw up, and then got up to go take a bath before bed.

***

The next morning, I woke up to a note from Seth saying he had an emergency meeting in New Jersey. I was slightly disappointed, but not as much as usual. I was actually kind of happy, because whenever he went to New Jersey I was free to do me.

I went to the bathroom to brush my teeth, and grabbed my phone along the way. There were messages from Madison and Aubrie, and then Yazir of course. I must admit, his refusal to stop pursuing me was really turning me on. I found myself smiling whenever his name popped up on my screen; even though I wasn't gonna text back. Today though, since my warden was gone, I wanted to respond.

Me: *Leave me alone.*

Yazir: *Nope.*

Me: *Being thirsty isn't attractive.*

Yazir: *I'm not thirsty baby girl, I'm determined and I always get what I want.* I smiled at his response and shook my head.

Once I was dressed, I went to meet my friends for lunch.

"So, have you been talking to Yazir?" Aubrie questioned as she bit her sandwich. We were at Corner Bakery in Manhattan Beach.

"I mean, he texts me, but I'm trying to make him understand that I'm not interested," I sipped my juice.

"You took Seth back?" Madison raised a brow and rolled her eyes.

"Yes," I replied begrudgingly. I knew they were gonna have a fit, and I didn't feel like hearing this shit.

"Ugh, why Nina? He is way too controlling!" Madison growled.

"Because I love him, and we're about to be married!" I rolled my eyes at her.

Whenever I told people I loved Seth, my stomach would start to hurt. The thought of actually being married to him never made me feel giddy or excited. Madison just shook her head at me, because she knew about my busted nose.

"I mean Seth isn't my favorite at all, but if you love him then it's cool," Aubrie sighed and drank her lemonade. "I would just love to see you explore your options though," she added.

"Thank you, but no thank you," I sat back in my chair. "So what's up with you and Sameer?" I quizzed, trying to change the subject.

"Well, he asked me on a date so we will see how that shit goes," Aubrie cocked her head. "But tonight, Yazir's best friend Dasey is throwing a party, and Sameer asked me to come," she added and she and Madison slapped hands.

"I can't, I-"

"Oh, yes you can and you will. Nina, just because you're engaged does not mean you can't be around the opposite sex anymore," Madison said.

"Aight, fine," I huffed.

I knew the two of them were hoping I somehow fell for Yazir, but it wasn't gonna happen. Even if Seth and I don't make it down the aisle, Yazir Willis was not an option. Damn, why was it so hard to convince oneself?

Chapter Three: Yazir

"You sure she's coming?" I asked my older brother as I fastened my chain around my neck.

"Yes nigga, Aubrie assured me that Nina was coming with her tonight," he responded and I nodded.

"Damn nigga, you ain't even smelled the pussy and you tripping," Dasey laughed with Sameer.

"I would love to smell that shit," I responded and they laughed even harder. "And kiss it, eat it, put some babies up in that shit," I chuckled with them.

"Damn nigga, what happened to you being a bachelor until forty-five?" Sameer frowned but was still smiling.

"Man, she changed all that. I had a fucking dream about her ass, and when I woke up my dick was so hard you could knock on the door with it. I had to rush to the shower and bust one before I got blue balls or some shit," I admitted and they cackled loudly.

"Her whole little crew is bad though. I kind of like that feisty one that be dancing and shit, but a nigga is not ready to work for no pussy just yet. I'm at a time in my life where I need to hit the first night and keep it pushing," Dasey commented as he brushed his waves.

"I was on that same tip until Nina's ass showed up. And the way she dissed me, man I loved that shit," I said as I tied my shoe.

"Ain't she getting married?" Sameer quizzed.

"She *was* getting married," I smirked and they both shook their heads.

Nina had me feeling beyond thirsty; a nigga was dehydrated, fucking parched in this bitch. I had never met a girl as beautiful as her. From her alluring cognac colored skin, to her sexy ass body and beautiful smile. The fact that she wasn't chasing after me like a little puppy was a major turn on, too. Her standoffish attitude alone made my dick rock hard. The night I have her legs on my shoulders, will be a cause for celebration; yeah, a nigga had it bad.

Sameer and I got into our separate cars, and Dasey rode with me. We were headed to Supper Club for Dasey's birthday party tonight. It was his twenty-second, and he was gonna do it big. I knew I should've been worried about turning up for my boy, but my mind was locked on bagging Nina. I just needed one night, and I was sure that she would never wanna be away from me.

Once we got there, the club was jumping and everybody was having a good ass time. The whole place was tinted a light purple, and people were standing on couches wildin' and all kinds of shit. Supper Club was the place to be if you wanted to leave with some for sure pussy, or if a chick wanted to get at a baller. Dream Bar was slightly more upscale, so you may not be as lucky.

I sat down in VIP with my people, and saw Matthew mean mugging me a little. I didn't give a fuck, he just needed to focus on getting my numbers up and not trying to have an attitude. See, even now he was worried about the wrong things. A nigga like myself would've been making sure I did all that I could to up the sales, or I would've been out hitting the pavement for another hustle. Matthew was a kept bitch and was not fit to provide or hustle. I felt bad for his kids and girl back in Mississippi. Shit, I even felt bad for that ferret he had up in my shop that day.

His baby mother Robyn was a pretty girl that got caught up with a dog ass nigga, who fed her bullshit on top of bullshit just to get in her panties. Now, here she was, twenty-four with four kids, and a rolling stone ass baby daddy. I shook my head and sipped my Hennessy as I stared at him pondering.

My phone buzzed and I saw it was a text from Gabriella. It was a picture of her in bed with this other chick named Olivia. Seeing them two tempted me to leave the party, but I had a greater goal tonight. A million hoes couldn't compare to Nina.

"They're here," Sameer tapped me, and I saw Nina walking into the area with her two friends. I put my Skittles down to prepare myself.

She was wearing a camel colored tube dress with matching heels. Her hair was down, and it looked freshly straightened. Her beautiful skin seemed to have a special glow tonight, and I wasn't sure if was her moisturizer or just my eyes playing tricks on me. I watched her walk in, and tried to clear my mind of all the dirty thoughts I had of her. Her friend Aubrie walked over to us, and Sameer, Dasey, and I stood up to greet them.

"Nice to see you again, Nina," I stuck my hand out to her as I towered over her. I gave her friends a quick, almost unnoticeable head nod before diverting my attention back to her.

"Likewise," she chuckled at me.

I sat down, and then pulled her down with me, but gently. She bucked her eyes at my aggressiveness, but I didn't care. I was becoming very anxious, and she was gonna stop playing games.

"Damn, you almost broke my arm," she grinned flashing her perfect teeth. I just stared at her, and she pushed her hair behind her ear to expose an ear cuff.

"I'm sorry," I said, and kissed her exposed shoulder. She tensed up and I smirked at her.

I really could not help it. I was hungry and she was sitting here looking like steak and potatoes.

"What do you want? I told you I'm involved," she said in a low tone and moved her shoulder back. A waitress then delivered the special cocktail that I assume she ordered prior to coming up here.

"Let me take you on one date baby, and afterwards I swear you won't wanna get married," I said and gazed into her eyes.

"Oh you're that confident?" she raised a brow and then mushed her lips together in order to keep her lipstick in place.

"Yeah, I am. I'm confident that I'm the nigga for you," I smiled and so did she. She was blushing a bit, and I knew I had her.

"Well, I'm sorry you feel that way, because I'm not going on a date with you. You're too young for me, and I'm not a cheater," she played with my beard a little, causing me to move my face closer to hers.

"Age ain't nothing but a number Nina, and there is nothing young or immature about me," I scooted my body closer to her this time. She didn't back away which was a good sign. I kissed her cheek, then her neck, and then her shoulder again. Her breathing became heavy as I placed my hand on the small of her back. "One date," I said as I planted kisses all over her sweet smelling neck.

"Where to?" she whispered. *Yes!* I thought.

I stopped kissing her neck and said, "Anywhere you wanna go."

"I want you to surprise me. Make it good since it'll be the first and last date," she giggled.

"Well in that case, I have plenty of shit up my sleeve," I bit my lip. I pulled her into my lap, and she tried to move but wasn't strong enough.

"Let me go, Yazir," she whispered and I shook my head no.

"See, you are immature," she smirked. This girl was so fucking pretty it was unreal.

"Insulting me won't get you out of my lap," I said and caressed her smooth thigh. It felt like butter or some shit. She just chuckled and then threw her arm around the back of my neck to get comfortable, before taking a few big sips of her drink. She may have been tipsy but I was not giving a fuck. I was happier than a witch in a broom factory right now, and I couldn't wait for this date. Once I was done with Nina, she would never wanna leave my side.

Just as I kissed Nina's neck again, my phone chimed, and when I peeked at it, I saw it was a text from Gabriella. I needed to figure out how to get rid of her ass ASAP.

"Designer" by Eric Bellinger came on, and by this time Nina definitely had some liquid courage. She was moving her body slowly, while singing along with the song. Although there were about fifteen of us in the VIP, my eyes were only on her. She had her eyes closed just grooving, and I enjoyed the show, still holding her in my lap. I kissed her supple cheek, and she just giggled while still singing the song. I was craving some Nina.

Chapter Three: Sameer Willis

I was high key excited to take Aubrie's fine ass out. I hadn't taken anyone on a date in years, so I wasn't quite sure what to do. All I knew was that women liked food, flowers, and wine, so I just put all that together.

Aubrie was beautiful, but her personality was what got me. Straight off the bat, I knew she was a wild one just by her mannerisms, and the way she talked to us when she worked our table at Dream Bar. I loved women who knew what they wanted and weren't scared to let a muthafucka know. If you were the timid type, then I wasn't the nigga for you.

I fastened my watch around my wrist, and then grabbed the yellow roses I purchased. After grabbing my keys and phone, I went and got in my Porsche truck so I could pick Aubrie up.

Tonight I wanted to be simple but still flashy. I liked to let niggas know that I was a boss, but in the subtlest way possible. That's something my younger brother Yazir and I had in common. We weren't the iced out from head to toe type, but you knew we had money by the smell of our cologne and the crispness of our shirts.

I peeled out of my driveway, and headed to Aubrie's apartment over in Gardena. It wasn't the hood yet, but it was for damn sure on its way. I got there in about thirty minutes since I lived in the quiet part of Beverly Hills. I checked my texts to see which apartment number she was in, and then walked over to knock. My mother always taught me to go and knock at the door, and not to send an *I'm here* text.

I knocked on her door, and as I was waiting, I heard Tamia playing from inside her crib. A few moments later I heard her unlocking the door, and it slowly opened as if she was preparing me for the greatness I was about to witness. She stood there in a light pink latex looking dress that hugged her curvy body, and accentuated her D cup breasts. Her hair was in a ponytail, and half of it was down. She had on big silver earrings, silver bracelets, and a silver necklace. I could smell her floral perfume immediately. She had some light pink heels on to complete her look, and her makeup was simple.

"Damn girl," I shook my head as I looked her up and down.

"Thank you. You don't look too bad yourself," she poked her big lips out. I had on light blue jeans, a white quarter sleeve button up, and white Nike Air Max. My dreads were hanging loosely, sweeping my biceps, and my neck and wrists were iced out.

"Thanks baby, these are for you," I handed the flowers over.

"I didn't take you as the romantic type, but I'm glad you have it in you," she smiled and took the flowers from me. "Come in," she said and then walked the flowers into her kitchen.

Although the outside of the apartments were pretty low budget, she had definitely upgraded the inside. I was liking her more and more, because there was nothing like a woman with style, and a woman who took pride in her appearance and surroundings.

"Let me just change my purse and then I'll be ready," she let me know before walking to her bedroom. I didn't know what changing a purse entailed, but I just hoped it didn't take long.

About ten minutes later, she came out with a pink purse that had a silver chain link strap. I got up and opened the front door for her, and then she locked it so we could bounce.

I drove to Paul Martin's in the Manhattan Beach/El Segundo area. It was an American food restaurant that I loved to go to pretty frequently. I liked this place because it was very quiet, so it was the perfect place to get to know someone, and that's exactly what I wanted to do tonight.

After pulling up to the curb, I gave my keys to valet, and then grabbed Aubrie's hand so we could go inside.

"Hand holding? I'm already liking this," she joked.

"I don't know what you thought I was gonna be doing to you, yanking your arm?' I looked down into her pretty face and she cheesed. Her smooth vanilla complexion seemed to have glitter on it, and it was a nice little touch.

After letting the hostess know I had a reservation, we were seated at a table in the back, closest to the kitchen. It was perfect because ironically, it was the quietest area in the place.

"I always see this place when I go to the mall, but I never stopped. I'm glad I didn't from looking at these prices," Aubrie bucked her eyes.

"It's pretty pricey for a first timer," I smirked.

"Oh, excuse me. I forgot you take women to fancy restaurants on the regular," she playfully rolled her hazel eyes.

"Correction, I eat at fancy restaurants all the time, but I don't take women," I said.

"Whatever. So when is the last time you took a girl on a date?" she inquired.

"Let's see, I'm twenty-three now, so when I was like nineteen going on twenty," I nodded.

"Wow, that's the last time you got some pussy?" She turned her lip up and then laughed.

"I think you know the answer to that baby girl. I don't take every girl that I take down out to eat," I responded.

"So I'm special then, huh?" She raised her perfect brow.

"Right now, yeah. We will see how long I keep you around," I said and she twisted her lips up like she was thinking.

The waitress walked over and took our drink orders, and then skated off to give us time to look over the food portion of the menu.

"So when is the last time you were taken on a date?" I asked before sipping my water.

"Well let's see, I'm twenty-three now, so when I was like twenty-one going on twenty-two," she imitated me and I chuckled.

"And what happened with that?" I questioned.

"We dated for a little bit but he was a liar." She cleared her throat, signaling that this conversation was uncomfortable for her.

"Oh damn, that's never good," I said and she shook her head.

"But, I'm happy you asked me out, though," she nibbled on her lip while holding the menu in her hands.

"Oh yeah? Why is that? Because I'm cute?" I grinned and so did she with her cute ass.

"Well that's a given Sameer, but because I think you're cool," she nodded.

"I think you're cool too, and sexy as hell," I licked my lips and she inhaled sharply.

"Is that what made you ask for my number?" She cocked her head, making the ponytail on her head sway to the side.

"To be honest, I saw your body and was like fuck. Then you showed your face and I was like I have to have her. It's rare that you see a beautiful woman that has a nice body too, without surgery. You haven't had surgery have you?" I furrowed my brows.

"No, everything on me is natural except for this hair in my head," she laughed and so did I.

"Well, I don't mind that, as long as that shit don't start smelling like spoiled milk," I frowned at the thought.

"What? That's happened before?" she leaned in and snickered.

"Yeah, that bitch laid her head on my chest and I almost threw up," I replied and she burst into laughter.

"You do not have to worry about that with me aight? I wash my shit, and I get it redone frequently," she said still slightly chuckling.

"Glad we got that out the way," I smirked as the waitress set down our drinks.

"Are you guys ready?" the waitress questioned and I looked to Aubrie for confirmation.

"I can't decide," she pouted, poking out her sexy lips. I wanted to suck on them muthafuckas, lip gloss on them and all; I didn't give a fuck.

"We will have the marinated skirt steak, medium," I ordered for us both, and then handed the menus to the waitress.

"Great choice, it should be out shortly," she responded and sauntered away.

"Damn, what if I don't like steak?" Aubrie sipped her wine.

"You should, it's bomb as hell," I intertwined my fingers.

"Don't be flexing your muscles and shit," she giggled, and reached over to touch my bicep.

"I ain't flexing shit. I guess it happened when I folded my hands together," I laughed.

"Yeah sure my nigga, but if you keep doing that, you may have a problem on your hands," she said.

"What kind of problem?" I inquired while squinting my eyes.

"Me."

"That sounds like a good ass problem in my opinion," I shrugged and took a swallow of my wine.

"I'm crazy as fuck though. I don't know if you're ready for that," she ran her tongue over her pearly whites.

"Even better," I smiled and she just shook her head while grinning.

The food arrived to our table about twenty minutes later, and just like I thought, Aubrie enjoyed every bite of it. We shared dessert because she said she was too full to eat one on her own, and then we left the establishment.

"Thank you for tonight," she reached over and lightly rubbed my cheek, once I pulled up to her apartments.

"No, thank you," I grabbed her soft hand and kissed the back of it.

I then got out of the car to walk around and open the door for her. I pulled my jacket from the backseat, and then threw it over her shoulders before walking her up to her door.

"So, does this mean I get more dates from you?" I asked as she stuck her key into the door to unlock it.

"Who said this one was over?" she looked over her shoulder at me, and then pushed the door open.

"Shit, it don't have to be," I rubbed my hands together as I eyed her body.

"It ain't gon' be that kind of date nigga, we can just chill," she chuckled and closed the door behind me.

"I knew that," I lied and nodded before sitting on the couch. She opened another bottle of wine, and then made her way back over to me.

Chapter Four: Nina Joy

A couple days later...

Tonight was the night I was going on a date with Yazir, and boy was I ecstatic. Seth was still in New Jersey, so it was easy for me to be able to go out and do whatever I pleased. I lived for times like these.

I sat down on my couch fully dressed, and thought about what I was doing. Here I was engaged to one man, and entertaining another. And to make matters worse, I was more interested in the guy I was simply entertaining.

I felt so bad after that night at the club with Yazir, because I was in his lap and letting him kiss all over my shoulders and face like he was my man. I think the only time we were apart was when I went to use the restroom. Other than that, I was in his lap the whole night. I loved that he made it clear to all the hoes around, to give him his space while with me. He wasn't even my man, but I loved his work ethic so far.

The worst part of that night, was that it didn't feel wrong. Never once did Seth and his feelings cross my mind. I don't know if it was the liquor, or if the attraction between Yazir and I was that strong. If someone had have come up to me and mentioned Seth, I might have asked who they were talking about. It made no sense that this boy had me somewhat gone, without even a kiss on the lips or a night out.

This date is just so he will leave you alone, I told myself. That's the only way I could feel good enough to go out with Yazir. Once this shit was over, he promised he would let me be, but I kind of didn't want him to. Regardless of what I wanted though, I was spoken for and he was too young. I was trying to convince myself of too many things at the moment, and it was not working.

BRRNNGG!

I jumped when my phone rang and I saw it was Seth.

"Hello," I answered.

"Hey sexy, how are you?" he said into the phone. Why did he have to be so nice right now? I really felt bad. But did I feel bad enough to cancel the date though? Hell no.

"I-I'm good, how are you?" I stuttered slightly.

"I'm doing okay. I would rather be laid up with you," he replied, and I just chuckled lightly because I didn't feel the same. I wanted to miss him but I just... didn't. "What are you doing tonight?" he asked.

"I'm just gonna go to dinner with Aubrie and Madison," I said.

"Oh really, okay. Well, have fun, sweetheart," he responded.

"I will," I sighed just as my other line rang. I pulled the phone away from my ear, and saw it was Yazir. "Okay, I have to go Seth," I said, and anxiously waited for him to say his piece and hang up.

"Alright, I love you, Nina," he said, and paused for my response.

"You... me too," I shot out quickly and hung up before he could reprimand me on my reply.

I snatched my purse and rushed to the window to look out. Yazir was leaning up against a black Range Rover, and I snatched the door open so fast I almost broke a damn nail. When he saw me, the cutest and biggest smile spread across his beautiful face. He was wearing blue jeans that weren't too baggy or too tight, black Nikes, a gray crew neck, and a black snapback. He was so sexy, and his aura was very alluring. Something about him always turned me into a magnet when he was around.

I closed my front door behind me, and then put the top lock on. As I neared him I couldn't help but to smile. It burst through my face before I could even think to stop it. Why was I so excited?

"Hi," I said bashfully.

"What's up, beautiful?" He got up off the car and towered over me for a hug. The feeling of his hard body against mine sparked all kinds of naughty things in my mind.

"I think I'm overdressed," I chuckled and gently stepped back from his embrace. I was wearing the short white dress that I had initially bought for Seth's event a while back. I wore white sandal stilettos to complete the look.

"No, you look good, very good," he nodded as he looked me up and down. It was already a plus that he liked my dress.

My hair was hanging down, and I had a deep side part with the swoop pushed behind my ears to expose my big gold earrings. Seth hated these, so I was never usually able to wear them anywhere.

Yazir turned around and opened the door for me, and then went to get in on his side. He reached in the back, and then handed me a bouquet of white roses.

"Do you even like flowers? I didn't ask," he laughed and then buckled his seat belt.

"Yes, I love flowers," I grinned and inhaled the scent of them. "Thank you, this was sweet," I tittered and he nodded to say you're welcome.

He cranked up the car and we sped off, while listening to some music. His playlist was all over the place. One minute it was Usher, and the next minute it was Problem. I didn't mind it though; I actually enjoyed listening to something that wasn't Seth's slow jam list.

We made it to a port with about three planes parked on the runway. One was black, another dark blue, and then a white one. They all had little accents of gold, and I could tell the insides of them were decked out. There was a restaurant at this port, so I guess we were eating here. We walked through, and then out to the back where the planes were, so I snapped my neck to look up at Yazir.

"Where are we going?" I quizzed just as the white plane's stair door came down, and a pilot emerged.

"On our date," he laughed at me and put some Skittles into his mouth.

"By plane though? Where-"

"You said to surprise you, now get on," he touched the small of my back and then helped me up the stairs and onto the plane.

Just as I had expected, it was decked the fuck out. The seats were all white leather, there was a mini bar, TVs, a computer, closets, beds, and the bathroom was one of a five-star hotel. We took our seats in the big plush chairs and buckled up. I stared at him as he continued to eat his stupid candy. This was the third time I saw him with a bag of skittles on hand.

"Why do you always have Skittles on deck?" I laughed.

"I love them so I buy the big ass boxes from Costco so that I never run out," he snickered and gestured to show me how big the box from Costco was. "Want some?" he offered, and I shook my head no.

After pouring some champagne and getting settled, we buckled up and then ascended into the air. I was kind of scared of plane rides, so I wasn't too keen on flying anywhere, but after about forty-five minutes we began landing.

"That was fast," I frowned as if I was bummed about the flight being over. Little did he know, I was happy as fuck we were on Earth's grounds again.

We got off the plane and I immediately recognized my surroundings. "Vegas, Yazir? What is wrong with you?" I laughed and lightly tapped his muscular chest. *Damn*, I thought. *Be good, Nina*, I told myself.

"Yeah, and here are some ones for the strip club," he handed me a little stack of ones and continued walking.

"The strip club? What kind of date is this!" I turned my lip up and stopped walking.

"I'm kidding, bring your high strung ass on," he cackled and snatched the little stack back from me.

We checked into this hotel named The Venetian, and I was excited to stay here. I always wanted to try this place out, but it was too damn expensive. When I came with Seth he didn't wanna stay on the strip, so this wasn't an option.

The suite, or should I say mini apartment since it had two bedrooms, was what I expected and more. This shit looked like it was fit for a king and queen. You could actually live in this shit and be just fine.

"I'm glad there are two bedrooms," I shot him a playful look, and he just stared at me with his arms folded across his chest. He was so fine. "What?" I asked.

"I love your personality. It's refreshing to be in the company of a woman who isn't falling at my feet," he responded and unfolded his arms.

"Women fall at your feet? Like in *Coming to America*?" I grinned and he nodded with a raised eyebrow.

"Shit close enough. I'm sure if I asked one of them to bark they would," he shrugged one shoulder.

"Even women my age?" I questioned and sank into one of the plush ass beds.

"Woman, you're the youngest I've been interested in," he walked over and leaned up against the wall next to me. "And we are in the same generation, baby. Stop acting like you're some cougar or some shit," he shook his head at me. I saw him glance between my legs since I was lying on my back. I was in no rush to end his viewing party either.

"For real?" I finally sat up with a frown.

"For real," he responded. "Now come on and let's go eat." He reached his hand down to help me off of the bed.

When I stood up we were body to body, and we both paused for a couple seconds. He let my hands go, and then wrapped his arms around my body. I felt like nothing could ever get to me or harm me while he was holding me like this. It was almost as if he was an actual knight from the fairytales. I reached up to caress his face, and he pressed his soft lips against mine. I felt an electric wave shoot throughout my body, and I immediately pulled away.

"My bad," he stepped back and then grabbed my hand so we could leave the hotel.

That small kiss was too much, so I could only imagine if we used tongue, or worse... had sex. I got more in that little peck than I ever have when I slept with Seth. How was this possible? I didn't even know this guy like that, and I had known Seth for over a year.

When we got out of the hotel, we got into a black truck that took us to Planet Hollywood. We went inside so that we could eat at this restaurant named Strip House. I could tell by the people eating here and the setting, that this place was expensive. Once we were seated, we immediately start looking over the menu.

"I definitely want a drink," I said as I scanned it.

"Me too," he sighed.

"Are you even old enough to drink?" I cocked my head with a smile.

"I'm old enough to do a lot of things," he gazed into my eyes. I crossed my legs just in case any of my juices spilled over, and then quickly brought my attention back to the menu.

"I think I'll have this," I pointed to a $3,000 bottle of wine and he didn't blink.

"I've never had that, but I will try it," he said.

"I was kidding. Its $3,000, I was trying to make you flinch," I smiled.

"Impossible," he chuckled and showed his pretty smile and extremely white teeth.

"Whatever, nigga," I waved him off. We put in our orders with the waitress, and she brought me my Tangerine Dream, and his old fashioned fairly quickly.

"Can I taste that?" I leaned over and he nodded before pushing it over. I sipped it and I swear I felt hair sprout on my chest. "Ugh! That is way too strong!" I frowned and gulped some water. Although a bartender, people never ordered those, and I had always wanted to taste one but just never got around to it.

"Grow up. This is a man's drink, baby," he taunted and I rolled my eyes playfully. "So where is your husband to be?" he asked and sipped his drink.

"Away on business in New Jersey," I shrugged for some reason.

"I bet you're happy as hell that he's gone," he squinted his eyes and sipped his drink again.

"No, I'm sad," I replied, and even I had to laugh with him at my dry ass response.

"Sure. I think you're happy he's gone because you wanted to come out with me," he said.

"Get over yourself, Yazir."

"I'm glad he's gone too, because I wanted you to come out with me," he looked into my eyes.

"Why do you stare right into my eyes like that?" I questioned.

"Because I'm talking to you," he chuckled.

"I know, but most people will look away occasionally, but you never break your stare," I said.

"I never noticed it, and no one has ever complained until now," he cheesed. "Am I making you uncomfortable?" he quizzed.

"When I first met you yeah, but now I'm getting used to it," I smirked.

Chapter Four: Yazir

"Well good, you gon' have to get used to me," I responded and she shook her head at me.

I could tell by how relaxed she was, that her man was one of those stuffy cats. She seemed happy to be away from him, like a bird finally set free or some shit. It was kind of sad, and it made me wonder why she was with his ass.

We ordered the Cider Glazed Scallops for our appetizer, and then the dry aged porterhouse for two. The food didn't take too long to come out, which made me happy because I didn't want her getting drunk from having no food in her system. From being with her at the club that night, I could tell she was a bit of a lightweight, and I wanted her to be alert for the rest of the night.

We said grace together, and then dug in.

"Oh my gosh, it's like butter," she closed her eyes as she chewed.

"It is good as hell," I nodded as I forked another piece.

"You've never been here?" she quizzed.

"No, I've heard about it though, so I thought I'd try it with you," I said and shoved some steak into my mouth.

"How do you know I've never been here?" she frowned.

"You don't get out much," I responded, pretty confident in my assumption.

"You don't know that," she turned her lip up.

"I can tell by your body language that you're used to being cooped up." I looked over her body and perfectly round breasts.

"My body language?"

"Yes. You're so relaxed, like you're free. You remind me of my homies when they first come home from jail," I smiled and she laughed.

"You're an asshole," she twisted up her pretty face.

"You look one-hundred times better than them though," I bit my lip and smiled. She blushed and she was so cute.

"Thank you." She took a swig of her drink, and then resumed eating her food.

"Why are you marrying someone like that? You seem like a free spirit," I dabbed my mouth with the cloth napkin. I had to ask her.

"Someone like what? You don't even know Seth," she furrowed her brows in confusion.

"I don't need to know him to see that you aren't happy," I said. I'd only been out with her for a few hours, and she was so much happier and giddy than when I first met her back at my club.

"You have to make sacrifices for love, Yazir. Everything isn't gonna be perfect." She stabbed her mashed potatoes in a slightly angry way. I knew I must've hit a soft spot, which only further proved me right.

"No it's not, but you should always be happy at the end of the day. Even when you go to bed mad at one another, you should still feel good about being with that person when push comes to shove," I told her and she just stared at me. Her brown eyes were so inviting and vibrant.

"What do you know about love?" She smiled because my eye contact and wisdom regarding her situation was making her uncomfortable.

"I know that it's supposed to make you happy. It won't always be sunshine and glitter, but it should make you feel good," I replied and she nodded slowly. "So answer my question, why are you with him Nina?" I repeated.

"Because he's good for me," she put some food into her mouth. She blinked repeatedly, letting me know how nervous she was becoming. It was almost like she was afraid for me to find out that she was not in love with the man she was to be married to. Unfortunately for her, it was extremely obvious.

"Is that what you think? Or is that what someone told you?" I inquired and raised my brow.

"Both," she lied, I could tell. It was baffling to me that she felt the need to lie. I was getting the impression that she felt some sort of obligation to marry this guy. Maybe he was blackmailing her. Shit I don't know, but I was not sitting across from a woman who was in love. I was sitting across from a woman who felt caged, confused, and unhappy... until tonight.

"Well as long as you feel that way, then by all means," I raised my water and sipped it. I wanted her to enjoy tonight, so I declined to continue questioning her. The last person I wanted her thinking about tonight was that Seth guy.

"I do," she spat and continued eating.

Once dinner was finished, we had to try their famous chocolate cake. We scarfed it down, polished off our drinks, and then hit the strip. We walked up and down it for a while, and it brought a smile to my face to see her so excited about being here. I grabbed her hand in mine, and held it tightly. She looked over at me, and then gave me a faint smile.

“Are you tired? You know we don't have to leave here until you're ready,” I said and kissed her temple.

“Stop kissing me,” she chuckled and flung her long ass Pocahontas hair. It was real too; I'd already low-key checked.

“And don't your feet hurt in those things?” I frowned and she shook her head no.

“But okay, we can go back to the hotel, I was just trying to walk off some of that food,” she patted her flat stomach.

“You don't need to do anything, you look good,” I squeezed her butt. I couldn't help myself. She didn't even jump or anything, which was a good sign.

I called my driver, and as we waited, I hugged her from behind and leaned down to kiss her neck softly. She placed her small hands on mine, and cocked her head a little to give me more access to her neck. My driver came too soon, and then took us back to the room.

As soon as we walked in, I only cut one light on so that it was still pretty dim. She sauntered in, and I just watched her sexy body as I closed the door slowly. Nina wasn't super thick, and she definitely wasn't skinny. She was right in the middle.

I walked up behind her, turned her to face me, and then dipped my tongue into her mouth. She started to push me off but stopped. I picked her up and she wrapped her legs around my waist. I pulled her dress zipper down, as we kissed heavily and hungrily. I put her up against the wall, and then let her down to pull off her dress. I dropped down so that I could get her dress past her feet, and once I did, I kissed on her flat stomach as she leaned against the wall. She watched me as I kissed all over her lower body, and pulled on her red thong. Once I got that off, I put one of her legs on my shoulders, and inhaled the scent of her center, while admiring the perfect wax job she'd just gotten. I pushed the leg up some, and then kissed her pussy slowly and softly. I sucked on her clit gently and she let out the softest moan. She tasted like unicorn tears or some shit. I stopped licking and sucking, and then pulled her into the master bedroom of the suite. I laid her on the bed, and then undressed down to nothing, before climbing into the bed with her. I slipped my tongue into her mouth and reached under her to unhook her bra. As soon as it was off, I sucked her nipples, and once I was satisfied, I kissed down her stomach until her pussy was staring me in the face. I pressed her legs against her stomach, and then went in for the kill.

"Oh my gosh, Yaazzz," she cried out as she massaged my hair and scalp. Her soft hands only made me go harder. She came and I just drank it up and continued to feast on her. I hadn't eaten pussy in a long time, and hers was a great welcoming. "Ugggh," she grunted sweetly as she released again. I let her legs fall back onto my shoulders, and pecked her lower lips lightly. "Oh, oh my gosh," she panted heavily. I reached up to caress her breasts, and then licked between her slit. She shivered, and her legs trembled on my shoulders as I got her high off my tongue game. I slowly began to eat her out some more, and made her cum so hard tears came out of her eyes. I got a condom from my bag, and then rolled it down as she watched.

"Damn," she whispered at my size.

"Told you I wasn't a little boy," I licked my lips down at her. She looked so fucking good, and I hoped the pussy didn't fuck my life up. I had a feeling it would though.

I lowered myself onto her small frame, and then placed the head of my dick at her opening. I put one of her legs on my shoulders, and pushed myself inside with force.

"Damn," I whispered, and I was only partially in.

Her pussy was gripping my dick like a muthafucka. She was soaking wet as well, and the feeling was euphoric. She flinched a little from the pain, as I pushed the rest of my ten inches into her body. As soon as I was all the way in, our lips crushed together, and we were kissing like maniacs. She whimpered into my mouth as I stroked her insides repeatedly. I could only imagine how good this shit would be raw. She put her small soft hands around my neck, as we sucked one another's lips. I didn't feel like I was fucking someone else's girl; I felt like I was making love to mine.

"What are you doing to me?" she cooed as I trailed my lips down to her neck. I pinned her hands above her head, and then flicked my tongue over her hard nipples as I plunged in and out of her. "Aaah, uhhh, aaahh," she cried out as she coated my dick with her juices.

"Fuck, Nina," I grunted. No woman had ever made me say her name. I wound my hips into her, and pushed her legs back for more access. "Your pussy is fire, baby," I told her, before kissing her passionately. It was so good I had to admit it to her. Maybe this is why that nigga kept her cooped up inside. I covered her breasts with my hands, and then began to go ham into her center. She was calling out to the high heavens as I sucked and bit her lips. "Ugghhh," I called out as I filled the condom up. I hadn't cum that hard in a while. "Tell me you're not getting married," I said as I humped her slowly.

"I'm not getting married," she replied and pecked my lips. She held it there for a bit, before her tongue made its way into my mouth.

"And whose pussy is this?" I questioned in between kisses.

"It's yours, Yazir." She looked into my eyes and that shit turned me on. I pulled out of her, and then kissed on her inner thighs and stomach, while she stroked my hair.

I hoped she meant what she was saying, because our little date had me on one. I would kill for her right about now.

Chapter Five: Nina Joy

Yazir had dozed off, and so had I after round two of our sex session. I'd just woken up in the middle of the night, trying to process everything that happened last night. I hadn't planned to enjoy myself that much, nor did I plan to sleep with Yazir. Did I regret it? No, and that was the worst part. I felt great, rejuvenated, and even more in like with him than before. I didn't feel like a hooker on the clock like I did with Seth, and that was strange. Someone I didn't know from Adam gave me more emotionally in the bedroom, than someone I had come to know over a year's time.

I sat up and looked down at him sleeping so peacefully. His dark caramel complexion was gorgeous, and his features were so perfect. His pecks and abs were flawless, because he wasn't too muscular and definitely wasn't skinny. His beard was lined up nicely as usual, and his kinky textured hair was always so soft like he had a conditioner from God in it.

I didn't know what was wrong with me. I had never become so enthralled and intrigued by someone so quickly. I was so interested in him; getting to know him and spending time with him. How could I do that with Seth back home? I wanted to run off somewhere with Yazir, but that was the immature way and I couldn't do that. In addition to that, I didn't want to give my poor mother a heart attack.

I looked over the tattoos that adorned Yazir's muscular chest and smiled. I was about to stand up, but I felt his strong hand grab my waist.

"Where are you going?" he asked me in a slightly groggy tone.

"Just to get some water," I replied.

He let me go, and I went to the refreshment area for bottled water, after slipping my dress back on. I gulped some of it down, and then walked back to the bedroom. I sat on the bed, and Yazir sat up a little to take the water from me. He polished it off, and I chuckled at him. Once he was finished, he reached under my dress to raise it up off of me.

"Why did you put this back on?" he asked as he pulled it over my head.

Before I could say anything, he pulled me down and got on top of me. He kissed me hungrily, and we proceeded to fuck all throughout the night. Is something really wrong if it feels right every time?

The next morning, we showered together, and then went to breakfast at a place called Bouchon, located in our hotel. We both ordered omelets with a side of beignets, and an assortment of pastries. I loved that we could pig out together, because Seth was always on me about my diet. He said he didn't want a fat wife down the line.

Just the thought of Seth temporarily ruined my mood. I felt like as soon as we went back to California, I would have to return to my boring ass life. Why couldn't I return and continue this illicit love affair with Yazir? I loved how intelligent he was, and I admired his work ethic.

He told me about how he made his way to being the owner of Blue Dream by the age of nineteen. It was unheard of for someone so young to own such a lucrative business, but he pulled it off. It was so attractive to me that he put his mind to something and achieved it. It inspired me to really focus on becoming a world-renowned bartender. Yazir said I could do it if I put my mind to it. It was a far cry from Seth's response, who said I just needed to focus on nursing or something more promising.

"So was I right?" he asked as he cut into his omelet.

"About what?" I smiled and bit into one of the pastries. I felt like I was in France.

"That after our date, you wouldn't wanna get married anymore," he responded as he kept glancing back and forth between his omelet and me.

"What do you think?" I raised a brow.

"I think I was right," he nodded his head as if he was so sure. He was so sexy and cocky, but not in an irritating way. His cockiness was well deserved. He stared into my eyes like always, and waited for me to answer.

"You know you were right," I sighed and sipped my juice. "I had such a great night with you. Maybe too good of a night." I shook my head and took a stab at my omelet.

"So, what does that mean?" he questioned and put his silverware down. I could see in his eyes that he was anxious. I could also see that he was just as hungry for me as I was for him. Unfortunately, we would both have to starve, because I belonged to someone else.

"I don't know Yaz, I can't just end my engagement. I don't even know you," I frowned.

It was the only excuse I could think of. How dumb did it sound for me to say, I really like you and love being in your presence, but I can't because I'm too much of a coward to the end the relationship I already have?

"Well, I know you very well," he grinned and I laughed. Flashbacks of us fucking invaded my mind, causing a few goose bumps to appear on my forearm and thighs.

"Not like that. But personality wise," I said. For some reason I felt like I *did* know him, and I liked what I knew a lot.

"We can get to know each other by spending more time together, Nina," he replied, appearing to be getting a bit frustrated.

"I can't spend time with you when I have a fiancé," I folded my arms. "Our time together ends here," I added before drinking my juice.

"Fine," he shrugged and bit the apple croissant.

He didn't say anything to me for the rest of the breakfast, or during the plane ride. When I did try and make conversation, he gave me short ass answers. When we walked on the runway to go back into the port, he didn't hold my hand like he'd been doing every other time we walked anywhere. I already missed the feeling of my small hand being encased in his strong one.

"How can you be mad, Yazir? The plan was for one date, and then we would go our separate ways, remember?" I barked once we got into his car.

Why did I even care? We were to never see each other again, so it shouldn't have bothered me that he was giving me the cold shoulder. I guess I needed something from him; anything I could get.

"You're right. I'm sorry, I'm not mad at you," he smirked and brushed his pointing finger under my chin.

"Well good, because you shouldn't be," I buckled my seat belt and he nodded.

He pulled up to the home I shared with Seth, thirty minutes later, and I was surprised to see his car in the driveway behind mine. Shit! Thank God Yazir had super dark tint on his windows.

"Thanks, I had fun," I spoke quickly and hopped out of the car.

Yazir just stared straight ahead and nodded slowly with his lips pursed. He was disappointed, and I could see it in his face and smell it in the air.

I slammed his car door, and his Range Rover peeled off before I even stepped onto the lawn good. I watched him drive away, until the sound of the front door opening snatched me from my thoughts.

"Seth," I smiled nervously.

"Hey sweetheart, where were you last night?" he questioned and frowned at my dress. *Madison or Aubrie, who should I implicate?* I thought.

"I went with umm, Aubrie, and made a one-day trip to San Diego," I lied.

"Oh, okay. I figured it was something like that. Come here and let me talk to you."

I walked inside, and he rushed me into the wall as soon as both of my feet hit the laminate flooring. I could still smell Yazir's arousing cologne. It had a calming effect to it, giving me a sense of courage against Seth. For some reason I felt he couldn't hurt me because Yazir had my back, regardless of the way things had just ended. I knew it was wrong to look to another man for security and protection, but I couldn't help my feelings.

"I swear you better be telling me the truth, Nina," he gritted.

"I am Seth, calm down," I replied dryly.

"Good," he smirked and then kissed and hugged me tightly.

Two days later...

Seth and I were having dinner at BJ's restaurant near the Del Amo mall. I could barely concentrate, because my mind was occupied with Yazir. I felt queasy at the thought of him hating me because I told him I didn't want to pursue anything with him. I wasn't trying to-

"Nina!" Seth yelled from across the table, making me jump and interrupting my thoughts.

"What?" I scowled because he was being over the top.

"Don't you hear me talking to you?" he frowned like I had two heads sprouting from my neck.

"Oh, no, I'm sorry. What did you say?" I pushed my hair behind my ears.

"What the hell is wrong with you? You've been in fucking la la land all night," he said through clenched teeth, while leaning across the table.

"Seth, what did you say?" I stared at him with an uninterested expression. I was so bored of his antics and he no longer intimidated me.

He sighed and said, "I asked you if you've ever had the beignets? It sounds good but I've never had it," he explained in a calmer tone.

"Yes you have, we just had them at-" I stopped myself, because I remembered it wasn't him that I had the beignets with... it was Yazir. He had seized my mind and thoughts.

"What?" he furrowed his brows.

"Oh no, that was Aubrie. She loves beignets," I giggled hoping he wouldn't try to investigate further.

"You know what, let's go." He slammed the menu closed, and then polished off his glass of beer. "Come on!" he barked as he threw a hundred-dollar bill onto the granite table.

I slid out of my seat, and he yanked my arm roughly. I tried to pull away but he had a very good grip on my bicep. I was so embarrassed as people watched Seth drag me through the restaurant like a disobedient child. This was just like the night of his event. He kept his painful grasp on me as we walked through the parking lot and to the car. He slammed me up against it, and then pressed his body against mine.

"Make this the last fucking time you have your mind on something else while with me! I am your man, and when you're with me I want all your fucking attention. I don't care if it's a man vomiting violently right next to you, I better be the only muthafucka you're thinking about and looking at," he hissed. My neck began to hurt from having to bend my head backwards in order to look up into his face. "Do I make myself clear, Nina Joy?" he raised a brow.

"Yes," I replied begrudgingly. He kissed my forehead as his eyes scanned the parking lot for nosey bystanders, and then he walked around to his side of the car.

I so badly wanted to fight his ass, but he may have stomped me out in this parking lot. And judging by the crowd's callous reaction to the way he'd just handled me, I knew they wouldn't blink if he did.

He may have thought he was keeping me in his clutches, but he was pushing my heart further and further into Yazir's hands.

Chapter Five: Aubrie

Sameer and I had been hanging out a lot, and I was really into him. I didn't wanna get my hopes too high though, because every time I did I would get let down. I've been in so many relationships that I've lost count. I have dealt with all kinds of situations from crazy baby mommas to psycho ass exes.

Dating had become such a stressful experience, that I just stopped fucking with people outside of Nina and Madison all together. I was still like that, but something about Sameer wouldn't let me pass him up. I was really interested in him, even though at first I just wanted some dick.

Sameer was gorgeous, and anybody that knew me knew I was a sucker for dreads, chocolate, and facial hair. Sameer had all three, so you know I was with it from the start. On top of all that goodness, he was cool as fuck.

Our first date was super fun, and he wasn't pressing me to fuck by the end of the night, which was a plus. He made a few comments here and there, but it was nothing out of the ordinary. I actually enjoyed his compliments and shit. It was nice to feel sexy, and to know that a man was attracted to you. And shit, as fine as he is, he may have been successful if he'd tried a little harder to fuck.

Tonight, he and I were gonna just chill and watch some movies. I wanted to feel him out some more, and make sure he was really something I should even be getting happy about.

As I was opening a bottle of wine, my phone rang and I saw it was Nina. I quickly stopped what I was doing and picked up, because I wanted to hear about this date she went on with Yazir.

"Hello," I answered.

"What are you doing?" she quizzed and I could tell she was smiling from ear to ear, which in turn made me smile.

"I am opening some wine, but tell me about this date, bitch," I chuckled and so did she.

"He flew me to Vegas," she paused and my jaw dropped.

"Damn, and then what? Keep going!" I said as I resumed twisting the bottle opener. She was only five words into the story, and I was already on the edge of my nonexistent seat.

"So he flew me in and we stayed in a suite at the Venetian, girl!"

"You know I approve of a nigga spending cash," I said. Seth's ass would've had her in some cheap ass motel on Paradise Road.

"Exactly. But anyway, we checked in and then we went to eat at this expensive ass restaurant named Strip House. We got full as fuck, and then walked the strip a little bit," she said and then stopped, indicating there was more but she was hesitant to tell me.

"And that was it? Did y'all kiss or anything?" I questioned.

"Oh my gosh!" she grunted and laughed. "We went back to the room and we fucked," she blurted and then held her breath.

"What!" I dropped the bottle opener onto the counter. "Nina, you are lying!" I bucked my eyes and stared at my cabinet as if it were her. She'd only been with two men prior to Yazir, and it took forever for her to do it with them.

"No, I'm dead serious. And he was not playing any games, Aubrie. As soon as we got into the room, he was pulling my dress off," she replied.

"Did you wanna do it?" I turned my lip up. I was hoping she didn't just fuck him because he wanted to do it.

"Yes I did. I came six times, girl. That young nigga can fuck and eat pussy like no other," she exhaled.

"You're only two years older than him, talking like you're thirty or some shit," I laughed at her.

"Whatever, and the dick was long and thick, bitch! I haven't been fucked that rough, or made love to like that in I don't know how long," she said.

"Wait, how many times did he fuck you?" I chuckled.

"Umm, twice, back to back, and then we woke up in the middle of the night and it was two more times, then we showered together in the morning and fucked again, so five times," she giggled. She sounded so refreshed, like she'd just come from a spa or something.

"Damn, so now what?" I put my hand on my hip.

"That was it. We're done. He said one date and he would leave me alone," she responded in a more somber tone. It was more than obvious that she was bummed.

"And that's what you want?" I frowned.

"Of course it is. I have Seth, Aubrie." I could hear in her tone that she was tired of me disregarding her fiancé.

"Alright, alright, my bad. I just think it's strange that you slept with Yazir so many times and so quickly, when you're supposed to be in love with Seth," I said.

"I know and I was confused too, but it's over now and I'm getting married soon," she huffed.

"Are you confused? Or just in denial?" I inquired.

"Neither anymore," she replied.

"You know you don't have to get married, Nina," I huffed.

"I kinda do. Hey, Seth just pulled up so I have to go. I love you," she spit out and then disconnected. I shook my head as I set my iPhone on the counter. I hated how Seth was more like her parole officer than her man.

I placed two wine glasses on the coffee table, and when I went to get the wine, I heard someone knocking. I set the wine bottle down on the coffee table as well, and then opened the door for Sameer.

"What's up?" he grinned. His dreads were in a ponytail, and he wore a Nike jogging suit with Nike slide-ins.

"Hey," I cooed and he slipped his strong arms around my waist.

I inhaled his cologne, and my clit tingled. I moved back so that he could walk in, and then I locked the door behind him. We sat down together, and then I filled our wine glasses.

"How was your day?" he asked me and squeezed my thigh.

"It was cool, just glad I didn't have to work tonight," I half smiled and filled our glasses halfway. "How was yours?" I asked.

"It was straight," he sipped the wine. "My brother, Dasey, and I just did inventory at the warehouse for Blue Dream, and then we went to a couple meetings. So all in all, it was a pretty boring day. But tonight made it better," he smirked.

"Because of me?" I questioned.

"You know it," he replied.

"So, what do you wanna watch? I have *Waiting to Exhale*," I joked.

"I think I will pass. I hate them women movies because y'all let that shit fuck up y'all attitudes," he cheesed.

"You hate those movies because it reveals how much men lie boo," I poked my lips out.

"I'm not the lying type. I have lied before, but I usually keep shit one hundred," he palmed his chest.

"Well that's good, because after my ex, I can't stand a lying ass nigga," I shook my head.

"What did he lie about if you don't mind me asking?" He sipped his wine some more.

"He got drunk one night at a strip club, and he ended up taking a stripper home. I guess shit got wild, and he ended up getting her pregnant. She confronted me when she was like six months along, and he swore up and down that he had no idea who she was and blah blah blah. Anyway, a couple months later the baby comes, and she serves this nigga, forcing him to get a paternity test. The baby was his, and that's when he told me the truth. He was still trying to be with me, but I was like absolutely not! And now he and the chick are married," I rolled my eyes.

"Damn, a baby? That's pretty heavy." He rubbed my back and stared into my eyes.

"I know, and after that, I was pretty much over being in a relationship. After a while, being lied to, cheated on, and all that shit becomes tiring," I exhaled.

"So what made you give me a chance?" He scooted closer to me.

"I thought you were gorgeous, obviously, but something about your aura reeled me in," I looked up into his face.

He paused for a moment, and then pressed his lips against mine. I set my wine down on the table behind the couch, and then cupped his face as our tongues wrestled. He reached under my shirt, and leaned me back but I stopped him.

"If I didn't want more with you, I would gladly do it, but I want to build something stronger first," I whispered.

"Sounds like a plan," he said before slipping his tongue back into my mouth. I had never kissed anyone for so long in my life, but I enjoyed every minute.

Chapter Five: Yazir

Nina was right, I couldn't be mad at her. I agreed to that dumb ass deal thinking that I would have been able to sway her, but I guess I didn't succeed. All that didn't make this shit any better, but whatever.

She had a nigga on the couch all night watching *Martin* reruns, low-key depressed and shit. I hated to fail, and this appeared to be my biggest failure yet.

I wasn't gonna give up on her, because like I said, I always got what I wanted and never stopped until I did. However, I was gonna let Nina think I was done with her. I knew she was feeling me just as much as I was feeling her, but it was time she did something about it. I was not gonna let her suppress her feelings for me just because she wanted to please her nigga. I was just trying to make her happy, and I knew being with me would do just that.

Although we'd only known each other for a short time, I was infatuated with her. I longed for her like an addict longed for his drug of choice. I don't know what she did to me in Vegas, or what type of spell she'd cast, but it definitely worked. There was no way I was gonna let her walk down that aisle, no matter what I had to do. Even if I had to pull a Dwayne Wayne.

"So are you ever gonna talk to me about where you were a couple days ago?" Gabriella pouted while trying not to cry. Here we fucking go.

"Fuck you questioning me for? Don't act like we spend every waking moment together," I frowned.

She was annoying as fuck. She showed up at my house fuming, and was now holding me up from leaving with her bullshit. I hated when she got in her feelings like this, because I've told her on countless occasions that we weren't anything more than fuck buddies.

Shit, not even that. We were just fucks, because she could never be a buddy of mine. I even went as far as giving her an option to stop talking to me in order to not get her feelings hurt. But every time, she would swear she didn't care and wasn't looking to be serious either. If that's the case, why are we standing in front of my gates having a one-sided argument?

"I heard you took some skank to Vegas, Yaz!" she screamed. I smiled at a neighbor walking by, hoping to mask my irritation with this girl.

"Bye, Gabi," I put my hand in her face and walked around her.

"You can't be treating me like this!" she hollered and hit on my back with her fists. I turned around fast as fuck, making her jump back so hard she broke the strap on her shoe, and fell onto the grass in her white shorts.

"Keep your fucking hands to yourself, aight?" I gritted in a low tone so only she and I could hear. She nodded to say okay as soon as the words left my lips. "Now the next time that you find yourself wanting to question me about some shit, you need to meditate or take a nap or something to change your mind. For the one hundredth thousandth time, I am not your nigga, I will never be your nigga, and I will never feel for you the way that you want me to. There is nothing you can say, and there is nothing you would ever be able to do to change my mind. You could rescue me from a burning building, and I still would only think to call you when I wanted my dick sucked. Does that clear it up for you? If it doesn't, you can repeat what I said to someone whose elevator has made it to the top floor, so that they can explain it to you in *nothing more than some pussy*, your native language," I spat and stood up straight.

She stared at me with a dumbfounded expression, and her face was drenched in tears. Her usual ability to stop them hadn't worked, and I didn't care. I was angry that she was bothering me with her bullshit, I was angry that Nina had played me to the left, and I was angry that my cousin Matthew had done nothing to change his fucked up ways.

I turned back around and went to my car. When I got in, she had finally stood to her feet, grabbed her purse, and limped to her car since she'd broken her shoe. I pretended to be occupied until I made sure she'd left, and then I pulled away.

I wanted to go talk to Matthew, because I had now given him two full fucking weeks, and his shit was not together. I pulled up to his condo on Lemoli, and parked in front of his door. I didn't feel the need to go to the visitor's section in the back, because this visit was gonna be short and sweet.

I pressed on the doorbell repeatedly, and that same hoe from my shop answered the door. Now, I was by no means the most faithful nigga, but the fact that he had this hoe all in his shit, with a girl and four kids back in Mississippi that he wasn't taking care of, disgusted me.

"Where's my cousin?" I asked her as I stared down into her lustful eyes.

She wanted some dick but she wasn't about to get it from me. All kinds of bitches chased me, and that meant I had the luxury of being picky. Unfortunately, she didn't fit the criteria whatsoever. And at this time, any pussy that wasn't Nina's made my dick turn its nose up. *Fucking Nina*, I thought and sighed.

"He's in the kitchen, but what's up with you, Yazir?" she grinned and folded her arms over her droopy ass breasts. She checked over her shoulder to make sure he wasn't coming, and then looked back up at me.

"Ain't nothing up with me," I replied and moved past her.

She jogged a little to catch up to me, and then started switching extra hard hoping I looked at her ass. It looked identical to a golf ball in texture, which almost made me throw up my lunch.

"Oh Yaz, what's up, man?" Matthew closed his fridge and set the bread and meat in his hand down.

The expression on his face alone told me he knew he hadn't been on his shit. I knew he thought I was just blowing smoke, but my presence here today proved his trifling ass wrong.

“Can you excuse us? I need to talk to my cousin,” I told Ms. Ratchet.

“Whatever you saying to Matthew you can say in front of me,” she half smiled and placed her arm on his shoulder. She then licked her lips at me, and motioned a blowjob since he wasn't looking. She really felt she was sexier than she was.

“Oh word?” I raised both brows.

“Yeah, me and Heaven are a team,” Matthew nodded.

She had the nerve to be named Heaven, walking around looking like Hell. I actually felt bad for Matthew's babies' mother Robyn, because she really thought Matthew was out here building for their family.

This light-skinned hoe, Heaven was sheisty, and he wasn't even smart enough to see it. That's one of the reasons I never gave Matthew a chance within my illegal businesses, because he couldn't spot a snake if it bit him in the nuts.

“Alright, Matthew. Bro, you fired. And when I fire you that means you cannot work for my blocks, stores, my club, or any other venture I have. Good luck with your future endeavors and taking care of this beautiful lady right here,” I nodded and then turned around.

“Wait, nigga, what? You can't fire me! I got kids!” he shouted and came from behind his kitchen island.

“Kids that you still don't send money to! Your girl hits me up every fucking month for some dough!” I growled.

I was paying Robyn's rent, utilities, car note, and putting money in my mom's account so that she could get his kids uniforms and Robyn some groceries. When I say this nigga wasn't sending a dime to his family, I meant it. He was down here living the good life on his Blue Dream salary, buying new clothes, shoes, jewelry, electronics, and blowing cash on hoes. He was literally paying prostitutes, which is probably how he met this Heaven chick. While he was doing that, his girl was down South getting eviction notices and having to wash their kids clothes in the bathtub. I refused to have her living like that because I loved his kids and she was a cool chick, so I sent money every month through my mom whenever she asked.

"Because I need to get myself together out here first!" he screamed one of his famous lies.

"Alright," was all I said before leaving. I said what I had to say, and he was done for.

We were still family, but as far as me helping him out, that was over with and I didn't care who had a problem with it.

"You shady as fuck, Yaz!" he yelled after me as I made it to his door to open it and bounce. His words didn't bother me because he was just a bitch begging for a handout.

I looked down at my phone once I got outside, and saw I had a plethora of texts. I saw Nina's name, and a smile spread across my face. I felt like a five-year-old on Christmas morning.

Nina: *Hope you had a good day, haven't heard from you.*

Me: *We've gone our separate ways, remember? Have a good night.*

I chuckled and threw my shit back into my pocket. It was only a matter of time before she came running to daddy.

Chapter Six: Sameer

"Have you told her yet?" Yazir asked me, referring to Aubrie.

"No, I haven't found the right time," I sighed.

"You probably should've told her on the first date," he suggested.

"If I had have told her on the first date, it would've been the last one."

I kept replaying Yazir's and my conversation from last night in my head. Suddenly, the sound of a dog barking snapped me from my trip down memory lane. It was my phone... again.

My phone had been ringing off the hook all day, and it was irritating the fuck out of me. I wanted to power it down, but I didn't want Aubrie to try and contact me and I not be available. She was coming over tonight for the first time, and I didn't want her getting lost or some shit.

We'd been hanging tough for almost a month now, and I was ready to take things to another level with her. I wasn't trying to get married or have kids just yet, but I wanted to become intimate. I wasn't gonna push it though, but I knew it was bound to happen soon.

My phone chimed, and I saw it was a text from Aubrie telling me she was in my driveway. I looked out the living room window, and once I spotted her car, I turned my phone off. I walked outside, and she climbed out of her Toyota Avalon wearing a smile.

"Hey, beautiful," I smirked as she rushed over and threw her arms around my neck. I pulled back and kissed her soft lips gently.

"I brought a bag," she lifted up a little overnight bag and smirked.

"Good, because I don't want you to go home," I said before grabbing her hand in mine, and softly kissing her again.

It was only around twelve in the afternoon, but I planned to spend all day inside *with* her and inside *of* her. I had no meetings to attend, and she didn't have to work tonight, so it was perfect.

I led her to the den, and then took her bag to my bedroom. I hoped she slept in here with me.

"Are you hungry?" I asked when I reentered the den.

"I am, a little," she shrugged.

"Do you wanna help me make some shrimp enchiladas?" I questioned.

"How do you even know if I can cook?" she quizzed.

"I don't know, which is why I said *help*," I chuckled and so did she.

"Of course, I'd love to help." She hopped up and then walked past me out of the den.

I watched her perfectly round ass in her jean shorts, and then licked my lips at how smooth her thighs were, and how sexy her back was. *Damn*, I said to myself and shook my head.

"Why would she wear something like that?" I asked my dick in a low tone.

Once we made it to the kitchen, we pulled out all the things we needed, and she ended up starting on some margaritas while I took over the food.

“So, what is your favorite food?” she inquired, while moistening the rim of the glasses.

“Shrimp enchiladas,” I snickered and so did she. “What's yours?” I looked over at her as she put salt on the rim of the cups.

“I love macaroni with lots of cheese,” she beamed and bucked her eyes.

“I'm gon' have to invite you down South for thanksgiving then, because my mother's macaroni and cheese is heavenly,” I said.

“What? You want me to meet your mama already?” she cheesed and poked her hip out. Her body was ridiculous.

“Maybe, maybe not. We have to see how you act.” I walked by her and squeezed her ass. My dick got hard immediately, so I knew I needed to back away.

We finished up in the kitchen, and then scarfed down the enchiladas and margaritas. I was paranoid about my phone ringing, until I remembered that I had cut it off. I didn't want anything interrupting what I had planned for the night.

“Would you like to watch a movie in my room?” I asked after I put our plates into the sink. She smiled at me for a little bit, knowing what I was up to, and then nodded her head.

I took her soft hand into mine, and then led her up the staircase to my bedroom. When we walked in, her mouth was wide open as she admired my room.

“Damn, okay Mr. Willis,” she looked around.

“I do what I can,” I shrugged and laughed.

I dimmed the lights, and then began to change into some loungewear. She watched me the whole time, and her stare was extremely lustful. I turned on my music, and "Ether" by Eric Bellinger spilled through my speakers.

"You gonna change too?" I asked. She stood up and removed her t-shirt to expose her red bra and toned stomach.

I walked over to her, shirtless, and then pulled her close to me. I dipped my tongue into her mouth, and began unbuttoning her little ass shorts. I couldn't get them muthafuckas off fast enough. Once I had them open, I pushed them down her thick thighs. She stepped out of them, and I turned her around so I could admire her ass in that red thong she was rocking.

"Damn girl," I whispered and she chuckled seductively.

She turned around and then pushed my sweats and boxers down. I stepped out of them, and she immediately got on her knees. See, that's my type of bitch. She slurped my dick into her mouth, and began bobbing up and down on my ten inches. She was deep throating it with no problem, and that shit was sexy as fuck.

"Shit, Aubrie," I looked down at her, frowning because it was so good.

Something had to be wrong with her, because so far she was a perfect ten. *Maybe the pussy is whack*, I thought. My balls started to tighten so I knew I was near explosion. She sped up and you could hear how sloppy the head was, which in turn made me nut. She swallowed and that turned me on even more, so I grabbed her up and laid her back on the bed roughly.

I kissed on her stomach as I pulled her panties down and off. I spread her legs, and thanked God that the pussy smelled good. I pushed her legs back, because I was about to get all in there. I began sucking on her clit gently, and she let out a soft coo.

"Mmmmm," I moaned as I made love to her center. I could taste that she took good care of her parts.

"Sameer," she called out and gripped my dreads. She started to push her pussy into my face, and I went even harder. I switched back and forth between dipping my tongue into her hole, and collapsing my lips around her clit to suck it. "Ooh, ooh shit!" she whimpered, and her body shivered as a river of her juices flowed into my mouth. I lapped it up, and then pecked the lower lips softly.

I opened my nightstand drawer to retrieve a condom, and then stared down at her as I rolled it down.

"I wanna get on top," she bit her lip with her adventurous ass.

"I don't think you can take all this dick on top just yet," I smirked. I was dead serious too.

She pulled my wrist, and I fell onto the bed with my dick sticking straight up. She mounted me, and then wiggled her way down. Halfway in, her face was already twisting up.

"It's some more dick girl, sit down," I gripped her hips.

She placed her small hand on my six-pack, and fell forward on me. Her body jerked very lightly, so I knew she was already getting off with what little dick was inside her. I sucked her lips and then rolled her onto her back.

"I told you, you weren't ready," I smiled. I put her legs on my shoulders, and then pushed the rest of my dick inside her.

"Aaah, aahhh," she gasped and bit down hard on her plump bottom lip. "Aahhh," she whined as I started to stroke her very slowly.

"You got something to say?" I raised a brow and grinned as I slipped in and out.

Her pussy was strangling my rod, and damn she was sopping wet too. I smacked the side of her ass, and she called out some more. She spread her legs even wider for me, and I started to play with her clit as I sped up.

"Shit, fuck," I cursed as plunged in and out of her.

"Sameeeer!" she cried out and twisted up her sexy ass face.

"Look at that shit cumming for me already," I said as I looked down between her legs. She was coating me, and the sight turned me on. I pulled her breasts out the top of her lace bra, and sucked hungrily on her nipples as I beat it up.

"Uuhh, uhhh, uuhh!" She was so loud, and it was like a beautiful symphony in combination with the sound of me going ham in her wetness.

"I'm about to nut, shit," I grunted. I kissed her sweetly and softly, while still fucking the shit out of her, and a few moments later we both exploded. "Oh FUCK!" I yelled and panted. She was out of breath as well.

I cut the lamp off, let her legs down from my shoulders, and then dropped down on her to tongue her ass down. She hugged my torso, and I could feel her heart damn near beating out of her chest. The pussy was phenomenal, and so far Ms. Aubrie was perfect for me.

Chapter Six: Nina Joy

Some weeks later...

It'd been three weeks since that little Vegas trip, and it was all I thought about. I fantasized every night about the way Yazir touched me and fucked me. I couldn't wait to lie down at night so that I could close my eyes and reminisce. Sometimes, I would even have an orgasm after just thinking about the things he did to me that night. The way he kissed every inch of my body, the way he sucked on everything from my pussy to my fucking fingertips. Yes, my fingertips, which he licked like they had hot Cheetos residue on them. It may sound like nothing, but that shit was everything. I think he just wanted to taste every bit of me, and that thought alone made my clit throb.

I hadn't let Seth touch me since, because I told him I had a yeast infection. I don't even think he could get me wet after what I experienced in Vegas. Also, I didn't want him ruining my memories of Yazir. If that was the last sex session I ever had, I would be just fine.

I was annoyed with myself, and the fact that I missed him so much. It was ridiculous because I didn't even know him! I literally met him, went on a date, and now I felt sick whenever I thought about him not talking to me anymore. I just wanted to see that sexy smile he always gave me whenever he saw me. I wanted to see his eyes light up, upon me entering the room like they always did. He made me feel like I was the best thing out there, and I wasn't used to that. Seth was always trying to change everything about me, and it seemed that I couldn't do anything right. With Yazir, he enjoyed everything about me. From the way I dressed, even to the way that I slept, he told me so. We knew very little about each other, but it seemed to be enough.

I put my hair into a bun, and rubbed my dream cake body butter all over my smooth mocha skin like I did everyday now. It smelled like carrot cake and I loved it. Not only that, Yazir kept smelling my neck when I wore it on our date. I was wearing it for him, even though he wouldn't be around anymore.

I slipped on my shorts and tank top for work, and then put on my work shoes. When I arrived, it was semi packed, but nothing special, which I was happy about. Although I loved making drinks, I hated when there was a rush, because I always spilled shit all over my arms and clothes, and I would go home sticky. The upside to a busy night was more tip money though.

I kissed Aubrie on the cheek as I was passing her, and then went to the locker room to put my bag up. I checked my phone to see if Yazir had text me at all, but it was just Seth saying we had another event he wanted me to come with him to. I rolled my eyes and put my phone up, before heading out to the floor.

I was so tired of these events that Seth wanted me to come to, just so that I could put on a show for his colleagues and their wives. I felt like he was depending solely on me to get a higher ranking.

After working at the bar for a couple hours, my manager told me there were two VIP tables he wanted me to work. I hoped it was some dumb rich niggas up there, because they always tipped heavily in order to floss. One guy gave me five hundred dollars once to impress some bitches, but then had the nerve to come back the next night asking for it back. I lied to his ass and said that I'd already paid my rent with it.

I prepared an ice bucket, and then went upstairs to drop it off and possibly take some food or specialty cocktail orders. When I walked into the VIP area, I saw Yazir, his brother Sameer, and best friend Dasey chilling with some girls. Yazir and Dasey were the only ones really flirting and shit, while Sameer was just chilling. I guess he and Aubrie were really into each other. It was good to know that she wasn't the only one serious in their little courtship. Aubrie deserved a good man.

I took a deep breath, and then set the bucket down on the table. I stared at Yazir for a little bit, and he glanced at me just for a quick moment, as if he wasn't just eating my pussy from the back, or massaging my feet a couple weeks ago. Yeah, I was feeling bitter right now and I had only myself to blame. But was I gonna admit that? Nope!

"Is there anything else I can help you guys with?" I questioned as my heart rate sped up. My stomach was knotted, and I wanted to cry a little bit. *This is what you wanted Nina, suck it the fuck up.* I told myself.

He just looked so good, wearing a crisp heather gray quarter sleeve button up, dark jeans, all white Jordan Retro 3's, with a blinding chain and watch. The tattoo on his neck of a ram, because he was an Aries born on April 16, was one of his sexiest attributes. His unblemished pecan complexion, and his beard were sexy as usual too.

"Can you bring me a Long Island Iced Tea, please?" The girl sitting in Yazir's lap smiled. Who was she? She wasn't even the same tired bitch he had shaking her ass in his lap the last time.

"We're out of Long Island," I spat before walking off.

I was so angry I didn't know what to do. I hated that I had to serve their table, because it kind of hurt to see Yazir be all up under some bitch. *How thirsty can you be, Nina? You just met the guy a month and some change ago.* I tried to talk down to myself in order to stop myself from caring, but that shit wasn't working.

After slaving for about two and a half hours, it was time for me to go on break, so I rushed to get my phone and text his ass. I couldn't help myself.

Me: *I see you move quickly.*

I waited my whole fifteen minutes and he never responded. The icing on the cake was seeing him on his phone when I returned to work on the floor. It was beyond evident that he purposely ignored my ass. *What if he hated me?* I asked myself.

I went up to his section, because I didn't want my feelings to cause me to lose out on money. I wouldn't dare allow any nigga to knock me off my square to the point where I would be missing out on my coins.

"Is everyone doing okay?" I questioned and looked around the section. I tried not to lock my eyes on Yazir and this new female in his lap.

"We'd like to order some food, please," Dasey replied smiling. For some reason I felt like he was laughing at my hidden pain.

"Sure," I said before taking out my notepad.

I took their order as I watched some girl kiss all over Yazir's neck, and him grab and squeeze on her ass. She was gonna have the time of her life with that dick tonight. Hopefully, she wouldn't get sprung like me. I ignored them, or pretended to, and then walked out to get the food.

For the rest of the night I played it cool, and he never texted me back. Nice.

"It's cool, I have a man," I said aloud to myself as I got into my car in the parking lot.

I pulled out on the road, and cut on my windshield wipers since it was raining. California weather was so bipolar. One day it would be hot as hell, then the next day it would be raining and cold.

As I drove home, I thought about my life and how I would be married in two months. I hated that Yazir had changed my mind about being married. I didn't want to get married at first, but now I was completely turned off by it. I didn't know if I could watch Yazir be with another girl like he was tonight. I wouldn't be able to sleep at night if I was married to Seth while Yazir entertained other women. I yearned for Yazir Princeton Willis.

I passed up my exit, and kept going until I reached the one to get to Yazir's house. I felt like someone was following me, but then the person exited the freeway. I guess I was just paranoid because I knew what I was doing was foul.

Seth had never been unfaithful to me, and I was practically running to hop on the dick of another man. To make matters worse, I only felt like I was cheating when *Seth* would kiss me or hug me too tightly. On paper I was Seth's, but emotionally I'd been Yazir's for a while now.

I finally made it to his house, and there was a big gate. I heard him give his address to the hotel clerk in Vegas when she was asking for information, which is how I knew where to go. I'm not stalker I just have a very good memory. My mom said I'd been that way since I was a little girl, and she hated it because I never forgot the promises she would make to me.

I got out and walked up to the gate to press the button. "Hello?" I heard his voice come through.

"It's Nina," I shivered as the rain drenched me.

"What?" he quizzed nastily.

"I forgot to give you something," I said. I heard him sigh and then the gates opened for me.

I rushed up the big ass incline, until I reached his door. I banged on his door until it finally flung open.

"What do you have to give me?" he stared down at me. His beard was so sexy. He was shirtless with a pair of gray sweats on, and the top of his boxers were showing. His six pack and pecks seemed to be protruding more than usual, and his caramel complexion looked lickable.

"I-umm," I slipped inside past him before completing my sentence, and there was a girl coming down the stairs.

I couldn't even speak so I just pushed his ass backward as hard as I could. He chuckled at me as he caught his balance. Here I was refusing sex with Seth, and he was slanging dick like a plug did drugs.

"What's wrong with you?" he grinned showing his perfect choppers, while stroking his beard.

The girl just stood on the steps in her tight ass dress. She was shaped like a trash bag of laundry, and her weave was thin at the ends, and higher than Mount Everest at the roots.

"I hate you! I thought I was different! But I see you just wanted to fuck me!" I screamed, making my throat become sore.

He blew out hot air, and then yanked me through the foyer and to another room. He closed the door, and then pinned me against the wall.

"I told yo' little ass what I wanted, and you said you wanted us to go our separate ways, right?" he stared down at me. "Right?" he yelled in my face and I nodded. "Alright then, so don't show up at my fucking house acting like I tried to play you or some shit. I told you I wanted you and you ain't feeling that, so miss me with the theatrics and the bullshit, Nina. If you wanna be my girl, then you need to grow the fuck up and be about that shit. But if you think I'm gon' sit here and wait for you to be a woman about your shit, then beautiful, you're sadly mistaken. I may be young but I ain't no fucking sucker. I'm a man regardless of what you think." He put me in my place.

"Okay!" I yelled back because I had nothing to say. He had me wetter than the pavement was outside in the rain right now.

"Okay, what?" he frowned in irritation.

"You can have me," I sniffled and wiped the tears that had stained my face just moments earlier.

"I can have you," he repeated and smiled at my choice of words. "You and that nigga are a wrap then, Nina. I don't even want you talking to him to tell him it's over. Someone else will do that," he said as he pulled my raincoat off.

"I can't-"

"It's that or I'm not fucking with you," he cut in. I was so turned on, because this guy that I had assumed was a little boy, was more man than niggas twice his age.

"Okay, but get rid of her-" he kissed me deeply, and squeezed my ass.

"Shut up and go upstairs," he said.

I turned around and opened the door to walk out of the room. I walked through the foyer, and old girl was still standing there. I walked past her up the stairs, and gave her a glare before making it up to what I assumed was Yazir's room. I heard her yelling a few minutes later, and then I heard the front door slam. I walked out of the bedroom, and Yazir was jogging his sexy ass up the stairs.

"Go in the room and take your clothes off," he told me.

I went into the room, and by the time I was naked, he walked in smoking a blunt. He stared at me as he took a pull, and then ashed it in the glass ashtray on the dresser. He undressed all the way down to nothing, and then walked over to me with his monster swinging.

"Did you sleep with her?" I asked, looking up at him.

"I was about to but I didn't get the chance," he smirked. "Come to the edge of the bed," he demanded. I sat my naked ass at the edge of the bed. "Take your hair down," he said.

I removed my bun, and let my long dark hair fall down my back. He walked up to me stroking his dick, then slipped it into my mouth, and I began to please him. I wasn't sure what I had gotten myself into, but it was worth the risk.

***

The next morning, I woke up around 9am, and he was still lying next to me. I rushed to take a shower and brush my teeth so that I could go to the grocery store. I was ready in thirty minutes, since all I had was my work clothes to wear.

I ran out to Ralphs grocery store to pick up some things I needed in order to make him breakfast. When I got back to his home, he was still sleeping, so his housekeeper, Brenda had to let me in. I prepared his breakfast, put it on a tray, and then took it upstairs.

"Rise and shine," I grinned as I walked into the bedroom. He stirred a bit, looked at my empty side of his bed, and then diverted his attention to the door.

"Good morning, baby," he replied groggily.

"I made you breakfast," I smiled and walked the tray over to him. He slipped out of the bed before I could sit it down. "Where are you going?" I quizzed.

"I'm sorry baby, I have to brush my teeth as soon as I wake up. I can't do anything before it," he chuckled and went into the bathroom within his room.

I sat there on the edge of his bed, and watched him brush and floss his teeth. He then rinsed his mouth with Listerine, and this was all done while he was butt ass naked. He looked like a Greek God so I didn't mind the view.

"Alright, I'm ready, what we got?" he clapped his hands together and I started laughing. "What?" he grinned down at me.

"You're not gonna put on any pants?" I inquired. He looked down, and then grabbed some pajama pants off the chaise lounge. "Better. We have French toast, your favorite, eggs with provolone, mangos, and papaya juice," I explained as I sat the tray across his lap.

"Damn, these are all my favorites, good choices," he beamed as he looked over the plate.

"I know, you told me when I asked what a great day for you would be like," I reminded him. He gazed into my eyes, and then nodded slowly as if he was remembering.

"Thank you for listening, beautiful," he bit his lip, and then said a prayer over his food before digging in.

I sat and watched him, and it brought a smile to my face to see him enjoying my cooking. I knew he was picky, so I was glad I passed the test.

"Usually I only eat my mom's French toast because everyone else uses too much egg, but this is bomb, babe," he said with a cheek full of food.

"Thank you," I smirked.

He looked me up and down while drinking his papaya juice, and once he swallowed he said, "We need to get you some clothes, huh?"

"Yeah, since you don't want me running into Seth," I rolled my eyes playfully.

"That's right," he chewed his food and nodded with his cute self. "I'll have a couple people bring some stuff, and you just take what you like. Who are your favorite brands?" he inquired.

Damn, so this is what it's like to date a boss, I thought.

Chapter Six: Seth Brooks

I sat in my living room sipping a tall glass of Gin. I'd been waiting all night for Nina to come home and she had yet to. She got off at 3am usually, and would be home by 3:25am, give or take a few minutes. The time was now noon, and she hadn't called or anything.

I'd been texting and calling her all night, but I got no answer. I became angrier as each hour passed. I'd been sitting in this same La-Z-Boy chair since 2:50am, and I hadn't planned on moving until I heard her car pull into the driveway.

Nina didn't know what was good for her, and that was our problem. She was young and dumb, and all I was trying to do was make her a more mature person. She may have been twenty-three, but she needed to act older if she wanted to be with me. She thought I was trying to control her, but what she failed to realize was that she had more things wrong with her than right. Like most women in their twenties, the only thing Nina could do well was lay on her back and open her legs. And she even ruined that by making me wear a condom and never wanting to suck dick.

So why did I want to marry her you ask? Because she was beautiful as hell, and I saw the potential in her. I knew once I snaked my way into her mind, gaining full control of her, I would be able to turn her into the woman I've always wanted. It was much easier to control younger women, because they were inexperienced and didn't know right from wrong. I was grooming Nina to become so dependent on me, that if I died she would have no choice but to do the same. See, once you got a person to realize they couldn't live without you, they wouldn't, and that's how I wanted Nina to feel about me.

I knew she'd been seen with some young guy, and people were telling me that it was the CEO of Blue Dream Rolling Papers. See how stupid she was? She wanted to chase after a guy who would probably get her pregnant with about eight children, and then leave her on welfare. Why do that when she had me? I was intelligent, witty, established, and overall a better choice for her. I guess Nina didn't want the lobster and steak she had in front of her. She was more interested in that McDonalds of a nigga.

She actually thought I believed her about that San Diego trip. It took everything inside of me not to knock fire from her ass when the words left her pretty mouth. I was a thirty-two-year-old army man, and bullshit never got by me. I never once stepped into that hole in the wall she worked at, but that night I did. I saw Aubrie working the bar, so she couldn't have been in San Diego like Nina had said. I knew because I never went to her job, she assumed that she could tell me such a thing. But I didn't mind stepping out of my comfort zone to get the information I needed.

I took another sip of my Gin, and pulled my phone out to call her again. After three rings, it stopped and went to voicemail. I called again, and it didn't ring at all meaning she powered it off. I laughed to myself because I was enraged. My skin was hot because my blood was boiling.

I had no idea where she was, but I was hoping she wasn't with that hoodlum. If she has given my pussy to his young ass, I will have to kill her. Just the thought of her being bold enough to lay down with him infuriated me. The fact that he may have possibly convinced her to slide up out of her underwear caused my jaw to tense up and my nostrils to flare.

I dozed off on the couch, and woke up at around 2pm. I checked my phone and Nina had yet to call me back.

"Aahhhhhh!" I hollered and flipped the end table over.

I threw the now empty bottle of Gin at the wall and panted heavily, as all kinds of thoughts ran through my mind. Was she out getting fucked right now? Was she dead? She better be dead, that's the only plausible explanation.

I quickly picked my phone up and dialed her mother Samantha.

"Hello?" she answered.

"Hey Samantha, it's Seth," I exhaled and ran my hands over my fade.

"Hi honey, how are you?" she quizzed.

"Umm, uh, not too good. Look, have you seen or talked to Nina? She didn't come home last night." I plopped down onto the couch, because I was tired of pacing.

"What!" she shouted.

"I know, I've been calling her all night and I got no answer," I shook my head.

"I'm gonna call her right now, and I will call you back," she assured me.

"Great, thanks," I huffed and hung up.

Her mother was always on my side, and I loved that shit. I could do no wrong in her eyes. Nina was always about pleasing her mother, and I knew Ms. Samantha would not approve of that thug she may have been chasing after. She would get in Nina's head, and then Nina would be right back in my grasp.

I placed another call, and waited as the line trilled.

"Daddy!" my son shouted into the phone.

"Hey son, let me speak to your mother really quickly," I chuckled at my boy.

"Okay, Daddy," he replied and I listened as he rushed the phone to his mother.

"Seth?" she inquired happily.

"Yeah baby, how are you?" I leaned back and sighed.

"I'm great, I just miss you," she whined.

"Well, as soon as I get everything squared away out here, I will be home to you and the kids," I grinned.

"Okay, I can't wait. I need you here to rub my belly," she giggled.

"Soon enough, sweetheart," I nodded.

"Okay, we will see you soon," she exhaled indicating her frustration.

"I love you M," I responded and then disconnected.

That was Maya, my babies' mother. I met her in my hometown New Jersey, and we've been together ever since. When I came out to Los Angeles for an assignment, I met Nina and I was immediately smitten. I planned to marry Nina, and then I would break the news to Maya and move on. I didn't wanna break up with Maya just yet though, because me and Nina hadn't walked down the aisle yet. As soon as we did, I would get her pregnant, and then send Maya on her way.

See, Maya was twenty-five years old now, and I met her when she was nineteen and I was twenty-six. I got in her head like I was trying to do with Nina, and she became my little slave damn near. I was tired of her now though, because she was starting to mature and think for herself, which I hated. If I wanted that I would date a woman my age. I knew sooner than later she would become a full on annoyance, so I had moved on to my sweet Nina. Maya was a thing of the past, or at least soon to be.

I hated to leave my son and new baby on the way behind, but I loved and wanted Nina. But right about now, she was gonna turn me insane if she had in fact run off with that little ass boy!

Chapter Seven: Yazir

I was in between Nina's legs, lying on her flat stomach while I caressed her thighs. I pecked her inner thigh and she giggled. She caressed my hair as I just stared at the wall, and inhaled the scent of her body butter with every breath I took. We'd just gotten out of a nice hot bath, and after spreading my favorite all over her body, I convinced her to lay naked with me. It was dark in the room, and the clock read 4am. The feeling of her soft hands stroking my short tapered fro, in combination with the warmth of her body, was putting me to sleep.

"You're mine," I whispered and kissed her stomach.

"For real or for fun?" she asked in a low tone.

"What do you mean?" I picked my head up to look at her.

"Like, we're exclusive, right?" she quizzed as she looked down at me, while caressing my beard.

"I wouldn't have it any other way with you," I responded and kissed all over her stomach and inner thighs some more.

"How can you go from living like a bachelor, to being a one-woman man?" she questioned as she rubbed my hair.

"I don't know but I'm gonna try," I answered. "I ain't saying I'm gonna be perfect, but I know I'm gonna make you happy," I added.

"I know," she said in a low tone.

"And you better not leave my side." I looked up into her eyes and she nodded with a smile.

"Have you ever been in love?" she questioned as she played with my hair.

"No," I answered. I was still lying on her stomach, listening to everything going on inside of her body. "Have you? And don't say yes if it was your fiancé, because that's a lie," I said.

"I have, once, when I was sixteen," she responded in a low tone.

"What happened to him?" I inquired. I silently hoped he wasn't around still, because I didn't want him popping up trying to steal Nina back.

"He died. He was murdered the night that I found out I was pregnant," she dropped a bomb on me.

I picked my head up and said, "You got rid of the baby?"

She shook her head no. "Not willingly. I lost if from stress. I cried every night for a whole summer," she whispered.

"Damn, I'm sorry to hear that, baby," I told her honestly. Although I wanted all of her love, hearing that she lost someone she cared for and miscarried soon after made me feel bad.

"It was a long time ago. I thought I would never be in love again, and that no one would ever compare to him. Seth just further proved my point. But then I met you," she picked my head up off of her stomach.

"You think you can fall in love with me?" I smirked and so did she.

"It's very possible," she nodded and caressed my cheekbone with her thumb.

I got up and kissed her lips, while spreading her legs some more. I put two fingers inside of her, and plunged them in and out.

"Mmmm," she cooed and tucked her lips in. I spread her legs even wider, and then sped up my finger thrusts.

"Uuuh, uuhh, aaahh," she called out as I fingered her and sucked her nipples. She was so fucking sexy.

I pressed one of her legs down, and went ham until she gushed on my fingers. I slipped them out, and then licked her nectar up. I rubbed between the slit, and my dick bricked up at the feeling of her wetness. She was still panting from our finger session, and she licked her full lips. I laid on my back, and then pulled her on top of me to ride me to sleep.

***

I woke up the early as hell the next morning, so that I could go meet with my team to discuss some things regarding my operation.

Contrary to popular belief, a lot of my clientele was coming from the white neighborhoods and prestigious individuals. I had lawyers, big time musicians, doctors, and all kinds of big wigs hitting my line for product, even police officers. They always paid extra, too, in order to keep their little habit under wraps.

On top of them, you had your usual drug addicts in the hood. You know, the muthafuckas who sat on the curb all day, in the same outfit they'd been wearing for a year, trying to conjure up a scheme to get their next hit. I served them all. Drugs did not discriminate.

I was making major bread, but I needed way more supply if I wanted to stay on top of my game. I'd been doing well so far, but for the past few weeks, the demand was outweighing the supply. Luckily, my supplier was able to give me more product. He had to cut a few people off, but he knew I was worth it. I made him the most money, and I was only in a couple areas around Southern Los Angeles. Because of my many other ventures, the legal ones, I didn't feel the need to occupy areas up north like Oakland and such. And even though I only reigned a couple spots, I was still known as the king, because I used a lot of elbow grease to make it to the top.

I walked into my warehouse, and made it to the back where I had a conference room set up. My people, including Dasey and my brother Sameer, were waiting there ready to listen up.

"How is everybody?" I asked and looked around the room. People spoke simultaneously, and asked me how I was doing as well.

I rarely had problems within my shit, because people knew I took no prisoners. If you fucked up you got fucked up, and there was nothing else to it. When I first started out, I had to bump off so many niggas who felt just because I was young, that I was some sucker ass nigga. They had to learn the hard way, but thanks to them, muthafuckas knew I wasn't the one to play with. However, there was one little snake in the grass that I planned to handle after this meeting. I didn't care if he listened in because it would be the last thing he heard while alive.

"Shipments will now be coming in every day, excluding the weekends. We're getting a lot of product out there, and I want to make sure we can always meet the demand. As you know, we've had a couple problems in the past few weeks because we weren't prepared. I don't want us weakening our shit in order to meet the demand, which is why I got us more shipments. Also, any police officers, doctors, or anything of that sort that want a hit, do not speak with them on any personal cell phones. Once you talk to them and square everything away on the dummy phone, burn it. To burn it, you need to call Xena, and she will do it from our computer system, aight?" I said and everybody nodded. "Each of you have six dummy phones per shift, so please only speak with three of these types max per phone before having it burned. Any more may give a snake time to catch you slipping. If you use all six of your phones, don't trip. These niggas are just as much an addict as the bitches you see scratching their necks and begging to suck your dick for something free. By saying that, they will find a way to reach you and purchase," I added.

"Alright, cool," they responded.

I went over some more procedures with them, and then dismissed everyone except this guy named Curtis. He sat there blinking repeatedly, and his forehead was drenched in this otherwise fully air conditioned room. His eyes darted all over the place, as I waited for everyone to leave. *Damn nigga, at least try not to look guilty* I thought. Dasey nodded to me, and then closed the door.

"So what's up, Curtis?" I questioned and turned my hat to the back.

"Nothing man, e-everything's good," he scratched his head and looked at Dasey. Dasey had no expression on his face.

"When did you get that watch?" I frowned.

He had a $5,500 Cartier watch on his wrist. It was nothing compared to $80,000 one I was rocking, but it was a Cartier nonetheless. It wasn't out of the ordinary for my workers to have nice things like that, because we made more bread than Sara Lee, but he bought that shit with my personal money.

"Oh, this shit, umm, like a couple days ago," he shrugged and touched the face of it.

"Curtis, do you like working for me?' I squinted my eyes.

"Yeah man, it's been really-"

"Then why the fuck would you betray me? I helped you because I thought you were a stand up dude, but I guess I misjudged you." I leaned back in my chair as Dasey cocked his gun.

Curtis' neck snapped in Dasey's direction, and his eyes almost popped out of his head. "Yaz man, I swear it was only a little bit. I only took a little bit of the product to sell so that I could spread the word about your shit," he chuckled nervously.

"That's the best you got?" I turned my lip up in disgust. "I don't need you to fucking spread the word about me. You know that, and I know that. Secondly, it's not your fucking job to be a got damn PR company. Lastly, I've been watching you for a week and you've been pocketing every dime on your Promote Yazir campaign. Where is my cut?"

"Uh, I-"

"Exactly," I said before pulling my gun out and shooting him between the eyes from afar. I had him thinking Dasey was gonna shoot him because I wanted to catch him off guard.

I was an excellent shooter. I learned at a young age how to shoot from my grandpa Otis. Every summer, he would take me out to the woods so we could hunt wild life. Over time, I became just as good as him.

Dasey opened the door, and my cleaning crew came in to get rid of Curtis. I shook my head as they carried him out, because he was dumb as hell.

After putting Curtis' stupid ass down, I decided to retire to my spot where I had Nina waiting for me. I hadn't let her go home yet, and that was how it was gonna stay for now.

I'd seen that nigga Seth blowing her up, and she hadn't answered just like she was supposed to.

Speaking of being blown up, Gabriella and Kiara were constantly hitting me up too, along with a couple other girls. I knew Nina peeped it but she hadn't said anything to me. I guess as long as it was obvious that I didn't and wouldn't respond, she was cool with it.

Chapter Seven: Gabriella Potter

Yazir had me so fucked up it was comical. I knew when I first met his young ass that I should've kept it pushing, but something wouldn't let me. He was so attractive inside and out, and I wanted to be on his arm.

I met him a year ago when he was twenty and I was twenty-six. He was younger than me, but he was very mature and masculine. One thing I love for my man to have is a super masculine attitude, and Yazir had that. He was a man's man as people say. Yazir was the type of nigga that could make a way out of no way. He was the type that if there was no food or money, he would do whatever he needed to do to provide for his woman and child if he had one. Yazir was the type of man who would give all of his limbs up, if that's what it took to protect his woman. That was something I have looked for all my life.

Every other nigga I dated has been immature as fuck, even though they were sometimes twice Yazir's age. Shit, I think Yazir and his brother were the last of the breed of niggas who would put their coat over a puddle for a woman. These niggas nowadays wanted *you* to open doors for *them*, and to pull out *their* chairs.

Although Yazir never gave me money, I still knew what type of nigga he was. He provided a sense of security despite what his I.D. read. I knew if I could get him to love me, I would never need anything from anyone; and I don't just mean financially.

When I first started dating him, my mother and father told me he would waste my time, and that he wasn't interested in anything serious at his age. For the most part, they were right. Yazir had told me on plenty of occasions that he was just looking to have fun, and that he probably wouldn't become serious with anyone until he was in his forties. I acted as if I was okay with it, hoping that eventually his mind would change. I knew that if I acted like a wife, he would make me his wife.

This whole year that we've been doing whatever we've been doing, I've been telling my family that Yazir and I were engaged. At first they were suspicious because I didn't have a ring, so I had to buy myself one. They were also eager to meet him, but that was something I just couldn't pull off. Yazir would never meet my family, and I didn't want him to either. As soon as they started asking about the engagement, he would shut it down. Yazir was never one to hold his tongue, no matter who was around. I loved his bluntness and arrogance. Ugh, he was so fucking perfect for me it was sickening.

"Damn girl, how long are you gonna be down?" my friend Chelsea asked me.

"I'm gonna be down until my man comes home to me! Or better yet, calls me home!" I snapped at her and sipped my drink. We were eating lunch at Red Lobster in Torrance.

She was trying to get my mind off of Yazir, but she should've known that was impossible.

"I mean, he ain't about shit, Gabi. He has fucked how many of your friends?" she turned her lip up.

"Only Kiara and Olivia, but it was a threesome, okay?" I frowned.

"And you honestly believe he hasn't got at them without you?" She stared at me and then laughed. I knew Yazir had fucked Olivia and Kiara without me, but I refused to believe it fully since I had no proof.

Chelsea was my best friend and I loved her. I hated her at the same time because she was that friend that would give it to you straight. She would never lie to me to make me feel better, because she saw no point behind it. She was the only friend that I hung out with still, because I didn't fuck with Kiara and Olivia anymore, unless it was in the bedroom, over of Yazir.

Kiara and Olivia both promised that they wouldn't catch feelings if I invited them to bed with Yazir and I, and they both lied. I felt like I was on one of those VH1 dating shows, because the three of us constantly bickered with one another, and were constantly trying to become Yazir's woman of choice, while he sat back and laughed at us. I knew he cared for me the most, but I wanted them to see that too.

"I don't know, Chelsea," I sighed and moved back so the waiter could set my pasta down.

"Gabi, you are a beautiful and successful woman, move on! He is twenty-one years old and he's already said he would never commit until he was almost fifty!" She shook her head at me.

"Yeah, but now he's in a full on relationship it seems! I mean, he's had little chicks here and there, but I was always able to get some time from him. Now? He doesn't answer any of my calls or texts, and I constantly hear about him and this girl Nina," I stabbed my food.

"Maybe Nina challenged him. You never did. You were too focused on doing everything his ass wanted and when he wanted. Men like a chase, Gabi," Chelsea bit into her lobster tail.

Nina, Nina, Nina. She was the talk of the fucking town with her whack ass. Yeah, she was a pretty girl, but so what! I couldn't understand for the life of me what she had done to make Yazir pine over her in the way that he was. She had to be practicing voodoo or some shit, because he was a whole new nigga.

"Yazir is not the type of man to chase a woman, aight? If you're not coming up out of your panties when he snaps his fingers, he's moving on to the next one," I explained to Chelsea's dumb ass.

She thought she knew everything because she'd been with the same man since high school, and now they were married. Her man was a square though, not an alpha male like Yazir.

"All I'm hearing are reasons why you should move on. You need a man honey," she cracked open a crab leg.

"Yazir *is* a man, he's a lot of man, too. I want a man that makes me feel like a woman, and he does," I smiled at the thought of him.

"Oh, and how does he do that? By sticking his dick in you?" she scoffed and ate some meat.

"That's part of it, but it's more than that," I huffed.

"Well, I'm telling you right now Gabi, get the fuck over it. It's nothing there and nothing will ever be there. Have you seen that movie *He's Just Not That Into You*?" She turned her lip up.

"If he wasn't into me, he wouldn't have been fucking me for a year!" I spat.

"If sex is all it takes to make you believe a man is into you, Gabi, you have a lot to learn," she shook her head and sipped her iced tea.

***

After having lunch and getting a little retail therapy with Chelsea, I decided to go home and rest my nerves. I wanted to take down a whole bottle of wine, hoping that it would make me temporarily forget about the man that I loved.

Some nights, I would wake up from a dream I had about him, and then sob when I realized it wasn't my reality. I missed him so much, and I was frustrated. I was frustrated because I had no idea how to get him on my side again. I was saddened by the fact that I had no control over the situation right now. I know God says to accept the things you cannot control, but boy was it hard.

I walked into my apartment with a bag of wines from BevMo, to see my mother, Carla, on my couch, filing her nails. She was such a girly girl. If she chipped her nail polish, she would repaint it right then, no matter where we were. One time she did it in the middle of the grocery store.

"Ma, what are you doing here?" I sighed and closed the door behind me.

"Gabriella, sit down," she patted the couch and then put her nail file up. I paused and threw my head back before plodding over to the couch. "Baby, what is going on with your impending nuptials?" she frowned and crossed her legs.

"We have to iron out the details," I exhaled and let go of the bag of wine.

"I told you I could help you Gabriella, and you said you had it under control. That was four months ago." She moved my hair behind my shoulder. I hated when she did that, because I didn't like my hair like that.

"Stop, Ma," I said in a low tone, and moved away from her touch. "Look, Yazir and I have it together. If I need your help, I will call on you, okay?" I massaged my temples. My head was killing me.

"Gabriella, we haven't even met this man. I'm starting to think something is not right," she said in her thick Spanish accent.

"Everything is perfect, Ma. Just peachy. Now," I got up and opened the door, "if you would please give me some space. I'm tired from trying on dresses all day," I lied.

"Why wouldn't you invite me or your aunt?" she folded her arms across her small breasts.

"Because I wanted some time to myself, okay? I didn't like any of the ones I tried on, so for the next fitting I will invite the whole clan," I exhaled.

"Okay Gabriella, but you make sure you-"

"Yeah, yeah, yeah." I didn't even hear what she said as I rushed her out of my door. I needed to get my locks changed.

I locked the door behind my mother, and then grabbed one of the wine bottles from the bag. I shoved the bottle opener in it, but I didn't even have the strength to twist it open. I stared at the bottle before falling on my side and crying hysterically. Lying to my mother only made me feel worse, when I came to the realization that none of it was true.

Chapter Seven: Aubrie

Sameer and I were at the Del Amo Mall in Torrance, because I wanted to shop at a couple stores now that it had been remodeled. I loved spending time with him, and so far, he seemed to be a perfect catch. There was one thing though.

Every other day or so, his phone would ring at about 2pm in the day. He would always get weird and either quickly deny it, or excuse himself to answer. I was trying not to accuse him of anything, because I knew my past relationships had me slightly paranoid. But you have to admit that shit is weird. A part of me wanted to ignore it so I could continue to be happy about our relationship, but that was just a teeny tiny part of me. The other 98% wanted to know who was always on his line every fucking day damn near.

"I wanna go to Kate Spade and see if they have a wallet," I told him and he nodded.

I looked down at my watch, and the time read 1:50pm. I wanted to see if today he was gonna get that call. I wasn't sure what I was gonna say, or if I was gonna say anything at all.

We went into Kate Spade, and I started looking around at all the wallets and purses they had in there. After a while, his phone rang and I checked my watch to see it was 2pm. What the fuck!

"I'll be right back, baby," he put his finger up. He walked out of the store, and stood in the foyer of the mall and began talking. *Should I walk out and eavesdrop?* I wondered to myself.

"Did you need help?" the associate asked me because I was holding a wallet, but paying attention to Sameer.

"No, no, I'm good," I half smiled and then began shopping again. I couldn't even focus on what I wanted, because my mind was occupied.

I mean, was I really in a place to say anything? It's not like he was my man or anything. Or was he? I was for sure treating him like he was my man, and he'd been treating me like I was his woman. You never knew with these niggas, though. They'll take you to dinner, buy you things, and move you in, but be floored when you start claiming them.

Just when I'd decided on a wallet, he came back into the store. "You find anything, babe?" he asked, and then hugged me from behind. "What's wrong?" he asked because I tensed up.

"Nothing, I'm ready," I said and moved his hands off of me. He took the wallet from me, stared at me for a couple seconds, and then walked it over to the counter.

"Ready?" the associate beamed and he nodded.

She rang us up, and he handed over his card to pay her. I was finished shopping for the day, because I just wasn't in the mood anymore.

"Only one store?" he asked me as I started heading towards the way we came in.

"Yeah," I responded dryly.

He didn't say anything else, he just paid attention to his phone while carrying my bag. I was walking far ahead of him, and he didn't even notice. We made it to the car, and that's when he finally picked his head up and put his iPhone into his pocket.

"Where do you wanna eat, baby? All the good places are over here," he said as he backed out of the parking spot.

"I'm not feeling well, Sameer," I sighed and pulled my phone out. I didn't have anything to do on it, but it could keep my attention still.

"What's wrong?" he quizzed.

"Who keeps calling you everyday at 2pm?" I looked over at him. I just couldn't hold it in anymore. Maybe it was good if he told me now how serious we were.

"Its business, baby," he shrugged and frowned.

"Business, okay," I laughed and groaned. A lying ass nigga made my skin crawl, and I had a feeling Sameer was one.

"What reason have I given you not to trust me, Aubrie?" He pulled over into the parking lot of Lucille's Barbecue. I didn't respond because I didn't have an answer. "You cannot base everything off of the niggas you dated in the past," he added.

"I ain't basing nothing off of anything," I replied with a slight attitude.

"Then why don't you believe me that it's business?" he inquired and I just stared straight ahead.

"I'm sorry, Sameer," I reached over and caressed his sexy face.

"You have to chill, aight? Ain't nobody tryna play you," he said.

"I know," I grinned and leaned over to kiss his lips. Damn, like the Mya song says *why you gotta look so good?*

"Now can we go have a nice dinner?" he looked into my eyes.

"Yes," I smirked and put my hand in his dreads.

"Good," he smiled and then pressed his full lips against mine. I closed my eyes to enjoy the feeling, and then a couple moments later we pulled apart.

We went inside to have dinner, and a part of me just couldn't stop thinking about who was calling him. I mean, what kind of business calls at the same time every day? Any other time he has a business call, he answers and talks right in front of my face. Why is it that every time this particular call comes through, he has to excuse himself and leave? But whatever, I didn't wanna keep accusing him for no reason. Right now I had no proof, and I didn't wanna lose a good man due to my paranoia. If something was not right, I would find out without having to snoop or search.

I was never the type to be looking in a nigga's phone and such. Information would always just fall in my lap, and I would know to move on. I just hoped that Sameer was being honest, because once I was done with him, there was no coming back. I don't care how many bouquets of roses he sends, and I don't care how much he begs and pleads. Once Aubrie is gone, she's gone forever. I do know one thing, with as much faith as I had put into this man, him turning out to be a fraud would surely hurt.

After dinner, we went back to his huge crib in Beverly Hills. I was feeling much better than earlier, and I was ready to get dicked down. We took our doggy bags to the fridge, and then he took my hand in his before leading me to the den.

"What do you feel like watching?" I asked and plopped down on the couch.

"Before that, I wanna give you something," he said and went into this little cabinet. He pulled out a blue box that was well known as the Tiffany's box.

"Sam," I whispered. A huge smile spread across his face, and he sat down next to me.

"Open it, Aubrie," he handed it over, and I just stared at him. "Open it, woman," he chuckled and I did so.

In the box was an eighteen-karat rose gold watch, with a black satin strap. I remember seeing this sometime ago and saying I wanted it, but I had no idea he was paying that much attention to me. The watch was over $20,000, and I never expected to have it in front of me.

"Are you happy? Mad? I can't tell," he said snapping me from my thoughts.

"Sameer, I can't take this," I said in a low tone, as I let my fingertip glide across the beautiful face of it.

"Yes you can, because I bought it for you," he reached over and pulled it out to put on me.

"No one has ever bought me jewelry or anything expensive before," I said in a low tone as I watched him.

"Really? Not a necklace or nothing?" he frowned and looked up from my wrist into my face.

"No," I shook my head. I didn't realize I had teared up, until he reached over and thumbed the lone tear away.

"Come here," he pulled me close, and then kissed me gently. "That's what I'm here for Aubrie, to show you things other niggas haven't been able to," he looked into my eyes.

I was at a loss for words, so he simply slipped his tongue into my mouth. *Lord please don't let him be harboring anything, I can't take it.* I silently prayed.

Chapter Eight: Nina Joy

Being with Yazir was like being in paradise, until I looked at all the missed calls I had from Seth and my mother. Every time I did, it snapped me back to reality real quick. I knew if I spoke to Seth, Yazir would go crazy, so I decided to just pay my mom a visit only. As far as Seth, I mean, I just really wanted my clothes from his house more than anything.

I climbed out of the huge bed at Yazir's, and padded to the bathroom for a shower. I loved his big bathroom, and his huge ass tub. I always felt like I was at a nice resort when I was able to take time and do bubble baths.

"Here are some things for you to start your day." Yazir's maid Brenda brought me a basket of things.

"Thank you," I smiled and so did she, as I looked through everything.

There was soap, towels, a toothbrush, mouthwash, floss, deodorant, and all kinds of shit. She brought me a new toothbrush every morning, because Yazir didn't believe in using one more than once. It wasn't a cheap toothbrush that hospitals give you either, it was the silicone one that cost about $100 a pop. He was so weird, but I liked everything about him.

Every morning after my bath, Yazir would have a rack of clothes for me to pick from. There were all kinds of shit on it from Chanel down to Levi jeans. I felt like I was shopping every day. Although nice, I still wanted all the stuff I had left back at Seth's.

I finished bathing and getting dressed in some simple jeans and an oversized oatmeal colored sweater, both from Levi, and then just brushed my long dark hair down. It was definitely time for a new press job. I took a deep breath as I finished slipping on some tan booties from Urban Outfitters, because now it was time to go and confront my mother.

I knew she was going crazy wondering where I was and who I was with. I'd been neglecting her because I didn't want to hear her judgmental opinions on my choice to be with Yazir. I wanted to enjoy my new life. I smiled at my thoughts.

Yazir's driver pulled up in front of my mom's house, and I quickly got out and walked up her walkway. I rang the doorbell, and then waited impatiently for her to answer.

"Nina!" she yanked me in and hugged me tightly. "Baby where have you been?" She kissed all over my face. "Seth and I have been going crazy looking for you, and Aubrie wasn't answering her phone either!" she squealed. I advised Aubrie to ignore all calls that my mother made to her.

"I'm fine, Mom, I promise," I half smiled and she let me go. She closed the door, and I sat down on the couch.

"Would you like some tea?" She asked.

"Yes please, jasmine if you have it," I sighed and set my new purse down next to me.

After a couple minutes, my mom returned to the living room with a tray of tea. She always put mine in a little kettle so that I could refill my cup when I wanted. After adding some honey, I sipped it and smiled as it went down. Tea could make any bad day good.

"Nina, where have you been?" she asked again and stared at me. She glanced at my new expensive purse, and I could tell she was surprised.

"Ma, I-I've been on a little vacation," I grinned.

"A vacation? With whom, Aubrie?" she inquired and I shook my head no before chuckling. I couldn't contain my happiness. It was bubbling over like a pot of stew. "Madison?" she questioned further.

"Another man," I smirked and sipped my tea.

"What the hell is wrong with you, Nina! You're engaged to Seth!" she gritted.

"I don't wanna be with Seth, Mama," I frowned at the thought of him. Seth was not an option, because Yazir already had me too far gone.

"What about your future? Who is this man?" she squinted her eyes. I could see the disappointment in them and it hurt me.

"His name is Yazir, and he owns the bar I work at," I responded.

"A bar? You left a man like Seth for some hoodlum who owns a bar!" She turned her lip up.

"He is not a hoodlum! Yazir is very established, he owns Blue Dream!" I shouted.

"The weed paper company? Ahh!" she yelped and placed her hand over her heart, before calling the Lord's name. "Nina, you go to Seth right now and you make up with him!" she screamed and grabbed on my arm, which I snatched. I was tired of everyone treating me like a fucking child. The only person who showed me any respect outside of Aubrie and Madison was Yazir.

"It's over between he and I, like it should've been long ago," I shrugged one shoulder and sipped my tea. At this moment, I didn't have a care in the world. It'd been a while since I felt that way.

"How old is this man?" she inquired.

"He's twenty-one," I nodded.

"You chose a little ass boy, who is probably only after you for some pussy, over a man who loves you?" She was so confused by my behavior. I could see it in the way her eyes searched my face. She was searching for a glimpse of the old Nina.

"Seth does not love me, he wants to control me," I said and set my mug down to refill it. "I want someone who loves me just the way I am, and naturally makes me a better person."

"Seth is trying to make you a better person, Nina Joy, and clearly you needed that," she scoffed.

"When he backhanded me, was he trying to make me a better person?" I raised my brow. In Seth's eyes, hitting me was a disciplinary act, and not domestic violence. That was a problem in itself.

"He apologized for that, Nina, and you messed up a really big promotion for him that night, he told me." She shook her head as if she didn't know why I didn't understand that.

"You know what, Mom, why don't you marry Seth? You seem to be very fond of him. As for me, I'm with Yazir and who knows, we may get married one day," I smiled.

"He is never gonna marry you, Nina. It's not gonna last, he doesn't even love you and he never will. You honestly believe a man with as much money as he has is gonna be faithful to you and love you? I brought you up better than that, sweetie. This is fun for him, and you're just another chapter in his diary and nothing more. He doesn't see a future with you now and he never will. It's not you though; it's him. He's twenty-one with millions maybe billions of dollars, and plenty women to choose from. Stop living in a fantasy and wake up baby," she patted my leg.

For some reason, what she was saying bothered me. I knew Yazir was no saint, but I hoped my mom's words did not become a reality. The way he touched me, talked to me, and overall treated me said the total opposite of what she was saying, however. Yazir cared for me, and way more than Seth ever did.

"Well, I would rather take my chances than go back to Seth. I don't want a man who hits me, and sees it as a spanking!" I frowned.

"It was once, damnit! Get over it!" she yelled. Seth had turned my mom's morals and pride to mush, and I'll be damned if he did the same to me.

"Yeah, and then as soon as we get married it'll be every night!" I shouted back.

"Who are you, Nina? You haven't even known this man for more than what, a couple weeks, and you're already acting like the common Los Angeles hood rat," she shook her head and chuckled out of anger. "He's gonna ruin you," she added.

"Well, at least I will enjoy myself along the way," I said before finishing off my tea. I stood up and headed towards the door, as my mother watched me with a perplexed expression. "Love you," I said before walking out of the door.

She hopped up, stood in the doorway, and watched me climb into the backseat of Yazir's black truck. I rolled down the tinted window once I was in, and gave her a sweet smile. I wouldn't dare let her know her words had gotten to me a little.

Yazir's driver took me back to the house, after stopping at this Peruvian food place named El Pollo Inka like I'd requested. Yazir loved that place, and I knew he would be happy to see I brought him some. My appetite wasn't as big, because my mother's words were stuck in my mind like glue.

The driver let me out once we got to Yazir's house, and I went inside to eat my food. Afterwards I fell asleep, but was woken up by a light shake. When I opened my eyes, I saw Yazir's gorgeous face smiling at me, making me sit up.

"I'm sorry I've been gone all day, but I got you something," he grinned and pulled a big box from behind his back. I opened it up, and it was a Ralph Lauren mixologist bar set! "This way when you're not at work, you can practice at home or wherever. I know you've been wanting something like this," he explained as I looked over the expensive set. It had to be about $5,000.

"Thank you, baby," I beamed and tilted my head back for a kiss. "I can't wait to use this stuff. Will you be my guinea pig?" I cheesed.

"What about Brenda?" he pointed behind himself, using his thumb.

"Yaz!" I chuckled.

"I'm kidding, of course I will be your guinea pig," he said before sitting down next to me and kissing my neck. "What did you do today?" he asked.

"Nothing major," I lied and smiled. "I brought you some food from El Pollo Inka." I caressed the side of his face, and stared at him as I thought about my mother's cruel words.

"Word, thanks babe," he grinned. "What?" he half smiled because I was still staring at him in silence.

"Thank you again for the set," I blushed.

"You're welcome, beautiful," he replied before kissing me gently.

Chapter Eight: Sameer

Two and a half years ago...

"What the fuck is going on? What did you do!" I screamed as I looked down at her mutilated body.

A nosey neighbor that I'd befriended, called me and let me know they seen a brawl going on outside of the building. I rushed over immediately, because I knew it was going to be some shit.

"She got what she deserved, Sameer!"

"What the fuck! You've gone too fucking far!" I gritted as I pulled my phone out to call 911.

Present time...

Today was gonna be stressful, I already knew it. I took a deep breath, and waited until the line of inmates started walking out into the visiting room. As soon as she saw me, a smile spread across her pretty face, and I couldn't help but smile back.

"Sameer!" she whimpered and ran into my chest. I hugged her tightly, and then we sat across from each other. "I missed you, baby," she sniffled and reached for my hands.

"Cherelle, how are you feeling?" I questioned. She looked the same, just a little bit thicker in all the right places.

"I'm doing okay, but I wish I could come home to my husband," she looked into my eyes lovingly.

"Let's not talk about that right now. You know that's a complicated situation," I patted her hand.

"It doesn't have to be though. You know I'm getting out in a month," she grinned and bit her bottom lip.

"I know. I'm happy that you get to come home and be free and shit," I chuckled and slid my hands from hers.

"So what have you been up to while I've been gone?" she cocked her head.

"I've been working as usual. You know me, Yazir, and Dasey have always been workaholics," I nodded.

I married Cherelle when I was twenty years old. I was talking to her for a little bit, not interested in anything serious, and she ended up getting pregnant. I only married her because her parents, my mother, and my grandfather said that it was the right thing to do. I didn't love her, but I did it anyway to make an honest woman out of her.

A couple months into the marriage, she miscarried. I saw it as a way out, but I didn't want to serve her with divorce papers right away, because she was already depressed over the baby. We decided to mutually part a few months later, and I began dating another girl named Lanae.

When Cherelle found out, she became angry and ended up stabbing Lanae to the point where she almost killed her. Cherelle has been in jail ever since, but she was to be out soon. I wasn't sure why she was still on this tip that we were some happy husband and wife, because we had separated long ago.

"Well I hope you're not still working too hard when I come home, because I think I'm ready for another baby," she grabbed my hands in hers again.

"Rell, I thought we both decided that it was time to part ways," I frowned and her smile faded.

"That was years ago Sameer, we reconciled," she chuckled.

"When?" I pursed my lips.

"When I was on trial! You got me a lawyer, and helped me get through all that shit. I thought-" she paused and stared into my eyes. "Who is she?" she wrinkled her lips.

"It's not about who I'm dating, it's about you realizing that our relationship is over," I sighed. "We both chose to separate, remember?"

"Is that why you don't answer my calls sometimes, Sameer? Is that why I don't get through sometimes?" she started to cry.

"Cherelle, baby, I need you to understand that when you come home, we will not be together. I need you to understand that we have not been together for a while. I mean, when was the last time we kissed or had sex?"

"It's because of the baby, isn't it?" she sobbed.

"No baby girl, it has nothing to do with you losing the baby. We were never like that and you know it. I liked you and you liked me, but we got into some shit that we never planned on happening. We were looking for a good time, and then next thing you know we're husband and wife with a baby on the way," I explained, trying to bring her back to reality. She wiped her face, and shook her head.

"Who is she, Sameer?" she quizzed. "I at least deserve to know who she is," she frowned.

Cherelle and I were more like homies than anything, so I hated that she was acting like this, tryna assume her position as my wife. As soon as she got out and on her feet, I was filing for divorce. I didn't want to do it now while she was in this fragile ass state.

"Does that really matter? What will telling you who she is do for you, Cherelle? All I'm gonna say is that I'm dating someone I really like, but even if I wasn't, you and I would never be." I looked into her eyes to be sure she understood. "And I need you to stop calling me every day damn near. A couple times a week is fine, but you're calling me like we're together, and I can't have that," I exhaled. She nodded slowly, and then sniffled. "And again, this is not because of her," I reiterated. "That's not to say that when you get out in a month that I won't take care of you until you get on your feet though, okay?" I added.

I didn't wanna tell Cherelle, Aubrie's name because she was crazy as fuck. I needed to make sure I protected Aubrie, because I didn't want another situation like I had with Lanae; especially because my feelings for Aubrie were much stronger. I prayed it didn't get to the point where I would have to choose, because Cherelle didn't deserve that.

I talked with her a little more to take her mind off of Aubrie, and it worked for a little bit. I put some money on her books, and then headed home so I could think and get some rest. I needed to be fully prepared for Cherelle's homecoming, and so did Aubrie.

Chapter Eight: Yazir

It was around seven o'clock at night, and Nina and I were leaving Disneyland and California Adventure. She wanted to go so badly, because she said she'd only been once when she was six years old.

At first I was dreading this shit, but it actually turned out to be fun; I wasn't gon' admit that shit to her though. What does my thug ass look like having a blast at Disneyland and shit?

My favorite part of the night was when we watched the parade, and how her face lit up at the sight of all the lights and shit.

"That was fun, huh baby?" she smiled up at me as we locked arms.

She had her extremely long hair in two braids like Pocahontas, and some sequins Minnie Mouse ears on her head. She was so beautiful even in the silliest attire.

"That shit was aight, I guess," I shrugged with a half smile and she nudged me. She was about to speak but her phone rang like it had been doing all fucking day. "Give me your phone," I said and she paused for a second. "Nina," I stared down into her eyes and stopped walking. I already knew who it was, because whenever it was Aubrie or Madison, she would respond right in front of me.

"Just give it some time and he will stop calling," she smiled and rubbed up and down my bicep.

"The phone," I put my hand out.

She smacked her full lips, and then went into the little bag she had to retrieve her phone. I clicked the home button to light it up, and saw Seth had called her forty fucking times. I had planned to send some of my people to get Nina's things from him, but I'd gotten swamped with work. I was already a busy ass nigga, and now that I had a girl, I was even busier. But now this nigga was interfering on my time with her, so he had to be dealt with.

"Just ignore him," she smiled trying to lighten the mood.

"Yep," was all I said as I handed the phone back to her.

We drove home, and I was so consumed with my thoughts, I didn't realize she was talking to me.

"Yaz! Hello!" she shouted and hit my arm.

"Oh, my bad, baby, what did you say?" I asked as I pulled through my big gates. I went into the garage, and hit the button so it could close.

"Nothing," she scoffed and folded her arms.

"Aye, calm down, I wasn't ignoring you on purpose," I squeezed her smooth milk chocolate thigh. I bit my lip as all kinds of thoughts floated through my mind.

"Whatever," she waved me off and moved my hand.

"Come here." I grabbed her chin so she couldn't move away, and pressed my lips against hers. She wasn't feeling it at first, but then her lips parted to welcome my tongue. As our tongues danced, I reached between her legs to feel her pussy through her jean shorts. "Fuck," I said in a low tone in between kisses. I immediately started unbuttoning them, and she pulled from the kiss.

"Can't we wait until we get inside the house?" she frowned.

"No," I replied being short, before slipping my tongue back into her mouth.

I yanked her shorts down, along with her panties, and then pushed down her tube top to expose her perfect perky C cups. I brought her over into my seat to straddle me, and then released my dick. I put her down on it, and she whimpered like a little puppy in the rain.

"Shit, Nina," I said before taking her nipple into my mouth. She grabbed onto the seat, and began to bounce up and down at a medium pace. "Yes," I grunted as she rocked her hips on me. Seeing her sexy ass body move up and down my dick, along with the faces she was making, had my dick on swole.

"I'm cumming, Yaz," she cried out as I switched back and forth between her nipples. I smacked her smooth round ass, and squeezed it roughly. I felt her release on me, and it made her pussy even wetter.

"I'm about to nut," I groaned as she dipped her tongue into my mouth. We were kissing hard as fuck, as she continued to bounce on my dick. "Uuuggghhh," I called out as I came all in her little body. We panted heavily as we kissed one another softly.

"I'm addicted to you, Yaz," she whispered as I planted kisses all over her collarbone.

***

The next evening, after eating dinner with my baby girl, I decided to go pay Seth a visit, unbeknownst to her. I pulled up to his crib in Carson, and parked across the street. It was a nice quiet little neighborhood, even though he lived on the borderline of Long Beach.

I only knew the address because I picked Nina up from here for our date. I laughed at the thought of me taking this nigga's girl just like I said I would. I was a little worried at first, but just like with everything else I put my mind to, I was eventually successful.

I ain't gon' lie, Nina had a nigga feeling like a kid in a candy store at the thought of her, and it was weird to me. Even the sex was different, and I think it's because I've never had sex with someone I had feelings for. The orgasms and experience overall is so much better when you and that person have more than a superficial connection. My grandfather and uncles always told me that, but I just thought sex was sex.

I went up the walkway, and then rang the doorbell. His Infiniti truck was in the driveway, so I knew he was here.

"May I help you?" he answered the door and sized me up.

He stood at about 6 feet even, and I was 6'4. He wasn't a skinny guy at all, but I was way more fit and muscular.

"I'm here to talk to you about Nina," I folded my arms. He stared at me with a confused expression, and then he chuckled.

"Oh, you're the little young nigga she calls herself leaving me for?" He came from behind his door, and folded his arms as well.

"Exactly, but ain't nothing little about me, little nigga," I scooted closer to him.

"Man, what the fuck are you here for?" he frowned and stepped back into his house a little.

I could tell what type of nigga he was. He was like vanilla ice cream with nuts. He was a boring ass, rigid muthafucka, but I could see that he was slightly off kilter.

"I'm here to pick up her things." I waved my boys in, and they barged inside to start collecting whatever looked like Nina's things. She had no idea I was doing this, so it's not like I could give them a list or anything.

"Aye man, what the fuck!" Seth started scrambling around trying to stop my men, but it wasn't working. These were some big body builder niggas, and he didn't stand a chance.

While he ran around his house like a chicken with its head cut off, I closed the door and made myself comfortable on his couch. He finally ran back into the living room, and stopped when he saw me sitting.

"That is *my* fiancée, and she is coming back, little boy," he grimaced. This nigga was so irate, that if you cracked an egg over his head it would immediately began frying.

"Let's get one thing straight, no part of Nina is yours, homie. Not that pretty smile, that sexy ass body, or that fire ass pussy. It's all mine, and I've been enjoying it for the last month," I smirked to piss him off. If this was a cartoon, you would see smoke coming from his ears right now. He charged me so I stood to my feet and pushed his ass hard as hell. "If you hit her line again, I'm gonna hang you from a tree by your intestines," I raised my brow as I stared down at him.

"We got all her clothes, jewelry, toiletries, and shoes, boss," my men let me know.

"That should be good," I responded and stepped over bitch ass Seth.

We walked out of the house, and Seth ran to the door and slammed it behind us. I shook my head at his whack ass. Hopefully, he wouldn't have to go out looking like he came from a cattle slaughterhouse, but if I saw his name pop up on Nina's phone one more time, that's definitely how he would spend his last day.

Chapter Nine: Nina Joy

Aubrie, Madison, and I were at the mall shopping for a few things. Yazir, Sameer, Aubrie, and I were going up to Santa Barbara just for a little couples' getaway, so I wanted to get some beach type attire.

Yazir was so different from Seth, in that he always liked to get out and do things. We were always making trips or going to fun places that I had no idea were in California. He had shown me all kinds of new foods and restaurants, that I felt like a foreigner in my own hometown. I guess because I was so used to being with Seth, and all we did was go to local restaurants or his work events that I dreaded.

My mom said Yazir's traveling bug was because of his age and immaturity, but I don't agree. I think it was a part of his personality. I liked to get out too, and since being with Yazir, I realized I liked traveling as well.

I would forget that he was younger than me, because he didn't seem like or act like less of a man than anyone else. We had deep conversations all the time, and he didn't make stupid jokes like most guys did. He was very mature for his age. Shoot, he was very mature for Seth's age. When it came down to it, Yazir was a boss ass nigga no matter what his age was, and I loved it. I still felt protected and secure when I was with him, and I never felt like I was older. Funny enough, it felt like he was older than me.

I knew my feelings for him were much stronger now, but I didn't wanna scare him off. So I wanted to wait and let him say that four letter word first.

"Damn, I wish I could go," Madison pouted.

"Why don't you come? I'm sure the brothers won't mind," I said as I looked around Free People.

"And be a fifth wheel? I don't think so," Madison threw her hand up and turned up her lip.

"I can tell Yazir to bring Dasey," I offered with a smile.

"I am no charity case, boo. I don't need you trying to stick me with one of Yazir's little friends," she smacked her lips.

"Little? How is a 6-feet-4 boss, a little friend?" Aubrie folded her arms as we both waited for Madison's answer.

Aubrie was right, Dasey may have been a lot of things, but little wasn't one of them. He was the same height as Yazir, and had the same lean but muscular build. He was kind of wild and out there, just like Yazir but times two, and I thought he would be perfect for Madison's crazy ass.

"Because I said he was!" she grinned and we all chuckled at her irrational ass.

"Do you wanna come or not, bitch? When was the last time you got some dick anyway? Maybe a one-night stand will get those panties out of a bunch," Aubrie offered.

She was always trying to get some dick for somebody. I remember for prom, she bought us all little gift bags with condoms, lube, and some fucking deep throat spray. None of us used it, including her, but she just loved doing crazy shit like that. I smiled as I thought about it.

"I'm good," Madison threw her hand up and switched through the store to look at the iPhone cases.

As I was looking for my size in a pair of jeans, someone bumped me.

"Sorry about that," she fake smiled.

She was the girl who was with Yazir at the club the night I met him. I remember her Nicki Minaj body having ass sitting in his lap like it was yesterday. I knew she didn't like me, because if I was her I wouldn't like me either. Yazir literally moved her out of his lap, just so he could chase me out of VIP and down the stairs.

"It's cool," I said and turned back to the pants.

"Aren't you Yazir's new little friend?" She cocked her head and moved her freshly done hair behind her shoulder.

I hated when hoes played dumb. Women paid close attention to everything, so when we say we don't remember a name of a bitch- we're lying. And right now, this bitch was fronting hard.

"Something like that," I said not trying to give her any information. She knew exactly who I was, and I'm sure this whole 'bumping into me' thing was no coincidence.

"Right, well enjoy it while it lasts girl, because Yazir is very spontaneous. One minute he is all over you, and then the next day he's on to the next," she shrugged and snickered.

"Well, you will be happy to know I am taking full advantage of my time slot," I winked. She glared at me, so I just walked around her, switching harder than I usually did.

I knew what she was trying to do, and I would be lying if I said it didn't bother me. She was obviously jealous, but women only got jealous when they had feelings involved. I had assumed she was some jump off, but maybe she and Yazir were more. What if she was his Nina at one point in time, but he got bored of her? Whatever the case was, I was not gonna fold in front of her ass. I will tell you one thing though, if he thought he was gonna move me out of his lap one of these nights to chase a bitch, he had another thing coming his sexy ass way.

"Ain't that old girl from Dream Bar?" Madison asked as she watched her walk out of the store.

Madison didn't like anybody, which is why she'd only had us as friends since I've known her. If you breathed too hard she didn't like you. I wonder what it was about Aubrie and I that made us stick. She was a great friend though, so I wasn't gonna complain.

"Yeah, who cares," I exhaled and placed my items on the counter.

"You better watch her, because she is dying to sink her crooked teeth into your nigga again," she rubbed my hair.

I tittered at Madison calling her teeth crooked because they weren't. She could always find a flaw, even if it wasn't really there. The person would always get pissed still, even though they knew they didn't posses the imperfection she'd just called out.

"And if he lets her she can have him," I raised a brow before handing my debit card to the cashier.

My bark was just a tad bit bigger than my bite, because as strongly as I was feeling about Yazir, I would be crushed. But I had to save face and make her think I would walk away shedding not one tear.

After the mall, we ate at this restaurant named Stacked, and then saw a movie since AMC was right across the way. One thing I noticed was that Seth hadn't called me all day. I wasn't complaining, but usually by this time, I would've had forty plus calls from him. The only reason I hadn't blocked him was because I felt bad for the way I left him. I felt he deserved more than just to hear it from my mother, but I didn't wanna upset Yazir. But I'm sure since Yazir sent some people to get my things a little while ago, he must've taken the hint. I just hoped he hadn't threatened Seth, because I didn't want any shit to be started.

I walked into Yazir's house, and as my heels clicked through the foyer, I thought about getting my own place. I was tired of living with a man, and then when it crumbled, I was homeless having to run home to my mom. I was gonna start looking for apartments on the low, just in case. I didn't wanna offend Yazir by up and leaving now. He may think that I didn't like being around him 24/7, and that was not the case.

I took my bags to his room, or our room, and then went in search of him. "Hey Ms. Brenda, is Yazir here? I saw his car in the garage," I smiled.

Ms. Brenda was a very skinny black woman, who could clean her ass off and cook some mean salmon croquettes. She had a deep caramel complexion like Yazir, and a short curly afro that she kept moisturized. She stayed in a pair of jeans, New Balance tennis shoes, white t-shirts, and a button up sweater.

"Yes, he's on the treadmill in the gym," she kissed my cheek.

I walked downstairs and towards the back of the house to the gym. I spotted Yazir running on the treadmill in incline mode. His shirt was off, and he had on basketball shorts and Nikes. I admired him as the sweat dripped off his petite nose. He was so fucking sexy, especially when he tucked in his full lips.

He looked over at me, smiled, and then slowed down to turn off the machine. "Damn you look good," he panted and wiped his face with a towel.

I had on high waist skinny jeans, a plain white crop top showing my stomach, and my long hair was pressed bone straight. I'd finally gotten it redone.

"Thank you," I chuckled. Him complimenting me never got old.

"Did you enjoy yourself with your friends?" he asked and sat down on the leg machine with his Powerade.

"Yeah, we shopped, ate, and then went to the movies," I responded as I walked into the gym. He was downing the Powerade as his flawless chest heaved up and down.

"Well, I'm glad you had fun. I see you're wearing the watch I got you." He nodded towards the diamond Cartier on my wrist, as he twisted the cap back on his drink and set it down.

It had both of our initials on the bands. He had a more masculine one with our initials engraved on it as well. I told him I didn't like rocking expensive things, but I loved this watch and the locket he also got me. I didn't like to connect real feelings with material things, but Yazir strikes me as the type to only buy gifts for a woman he was extremely fond of.

"Yeah, I saw your ex today," I said and sat down on the weight lifting machine across from him. I wanted to see if I got a reaction out of him.

"Oh yeah? Who is my ex?" he panted as he lifted the weights with his legs.

"The girl that was with you when I met you. She told me how much of a player you are," I chuckled nervously, while watching his face for any shifts in expressions.

"Oh her, that ain't my ex, baby. That was some pussy," he said it like it was nothing.

He said it like he was telling me what he ate for lunch. I mean, I didn't expect him to say he loved her, especially because he said he'd never been in love, but damn.

"And what am I?" I smiled and walked over to him. I hoped he said something to make me feel better about the way that jump off had me feeling.

"You're my baby, and my actual girl," he pulled me down onto him.

"Ugh Yaz, I don't want your sweat on me," I whined as he kissed on my neck, and slipped his hand down the back of my pants.

"You don't mind my sweat when I'm inside you," he whispered as he nibbled on my ear, and started to unbutton my jeans.

He knew nibbling on my ear, or kissing on my neck always got me in the mood. From the first night we had sex, he was always able to find spots I didn't even know I had.

"Yaz, I wanna talk about that girl," I said as he pulled on my jeans. He'd gotten one side of them just past my hip, and started to kiss my tattoo there that read *Paradise*.

"And I don't. I told you she wasn't anybody and she still isn't. Now quit running your mouth so I can get some pussy." He picked his head up and sucked on my lips.

He got my pants and panties off, and then propped me up so he could eat my pussy. It was crazy how the back of my thighs fit almost perfectly in his hands, as he pushed them towards my stomach.

"It's so pretty," he moaned as he planted kisses on my lower lips. I threw my head back once his tongue started to slowly flick over my clit, forgetting all about old girl.

Chapter Nine: Yazir

Two weeks later...

We were going to Santa Barbara this evening, but before I left I wanted to talk to Gabriella. She'd been calling me a lot, and had showed up to my house more times than she should've been. She scratched up my security guard's face, which pissed me off, but now that I knew she was possibly trying to stir some shit up with Nina, she needed to be dealt with.

I really had no idea what the fuck was wrong with her. I'd told her in more ways than one that I was never gonna fuck with her no matter what. But I guess when one is determined, nothing can change their mind. However, this evening, she'd better take this warning with more than a grain of salt, because I was ready to pull the chopper out on her.

I knocked on her apartment door and waited for her to answer. I'd text her earlier and she said she would be home. She lived in these nice apartment buildings in Torrance, which wasn't odd since she had a cool little job as a department store district manager.

"Hey," she answered the door wearing a robe. I scoffed and shook my head before walking in. She had soft music playing, but I was not falling for this shit.

"Look Gabriella-"

"Give me one second," she cut in and walked to the back of her apartment.

I sat down on her couch, and waited for her to come back. I took in the scenery of her little place as I waited. I saw a couple fast food drink cups in different areas around the room, which made me turn my lip up. A nasty woman was worse than anything. I'll take a broke bitch before a nasty one.

After a couple minutes I got annoyed and decided to go find her ass. I made sure my piece was secured in case she tried to set me up or some shit. I walked up to her bedroom and opened the door. Kiara was laid back on the bed, letting Gabriella eat her pussy like she was licking for gold. My dick immediately got hard, but I refused to fall for this shit. I couldn't fall for this shit.

They sat up when they saw me, and smiles spread across their pretty ass faces. "Gabi, come out to the living room, I need to talk to you," I said when she got up from the bed.

She walked over to me, and dropped down to her knees. My breathing became heavy as she unbuttoned my pants, and my dick got harder. Kiara walked over and put her hands under my shirt to remove it, and once my shirt was off, she joined Gabriella by getting on her knees. Kiara took my dick into her mouth, while Gabriella licked and sucked on my balls.

"Shit," I moaned. The only thing on my mind right now was bursting a nut.

They kept going until I pulled out and burst all over both of their collarbones. I stepped out of my jeans and boxers, and then directed them over to the bed. I bent Kiara over, and rolled a condom down before sliding inside her from behind. Gabriella laid down while Kiara ate her pussy, and that shit was so fucking sexy.

"Aaahh, uuhh, uuhh," Kiara called out as I fucked her silly.

Gabriella pushed her head back down between her legs so she could continue pleasing her. They both came hard, and then I laid on my back so Gabriella could ride me. Kiara licked my balls as Gabriella rocked her hips on me, and damn this was the shit. Fifteen minutes later, we all exploded, and I was spent. They fell to the side of me as we all tried to catch our breath.

As soon as that orgasm left my body, my conscience returned, and damn was it guilty. I tried to gather my thoughts, and make sense of what the fuck I just did. I just may have sacrificed the girl of my dreams over a half hour of pleasure. It's crazy how your judgment can become so cloudy as a man, when pussy is staring you in the face. The saying think with your other head definitely makes sense now.

I've never had to think twice when presented with pussy on a platter. It was always a no brainer for me to hop in it. But now, things in my life were different and I couldn't react the same. *Fuck!* I thought.

After a couple minutes of pondering, I sat up, removed the condom and said, "Gabi, if you see Nina out, don't say nothing. And don't hit me up no more after this, aight?" I looked over at her and I could see she was confused.

"Yazir-" tears started to stream.

"If you say anything, I mean even the slightest salutation to Nina, I will cut off all your limbs, and hang you by your neck to bleed to death," I hissed and meant every word. "Alright?" I raised a brow as Kiara watched Gabriella with a smirk. Kiara knew better so I never had to worry about her. But if she got petty, she would get that same butcher style treatment.

"But-"

"Alright!" I yelled and Gabriella nodded.

I kissed Kiara on the forehead, and then grabbed my clothes. I cleaned myself up in the bathroom, and then quickly got dressed.

Once I was good to go, I went down to my G-Wagon and drove home. I felt bad as fuck and had no idea what to do. Nina could never find this shit out, because I knew she was already weary of me. If she found out I cheated on her this early into the relationship, she would flip. And if she left me a nigga would be weak. Ain't it crazy how we do shit, knowing that if a person left us we'd be sick?

I pulled up to my crib, and parked right in front in the roundabout driveway. I sniffed my clothes to make sure no perfume was there. I then pulled down my visor mirror to make sure no lipstick stains were on my collar. I knew there probably wasn't because I don't remember either woman having on lipstick, but I was on some OCD shit right now.

When I walked in, I saw Nina's bags for the trip to Santa Barbara, sitting at the bottom of the stairs. As soon as I closed the front door, she came from the bedroom wearing black tights and a navy crop top. Her dark hair was in a huge bun on top of her head, and her cognac colored skin was glowing. She was so fucking beautiful, and her slim thick body was sent straight from heaven.

"Yazir, we were supposed to leave twenty minutes ago, where were you?" she asked and descended the stairs.

"Oh, I just went to handle some shit baby, I'm sorry," I said before pulling her close and kissing her lips.

"Well, Aubrie and your brother are already on the road, so we should go," she turned around and started to walk off.

I grabbed her from behind, and hugged her tightly. I let my hands roam all over her body, as I kissed on the side of her face and neck.

"You are so sexy to me," I said in a low tone. Before she could speak I had my tongue down her throat.

"Yaz, we have to go," she whined in between kisses.

"Aight," I let her go. If I hadn't just fucked them hoes, I would've beat it up right here on the stairs, but I couldn't do that. Shit.

I rushed upstairs to take a scalding hot shower, and scrubbed my skin until it was red. Nina was pissed that I wanted to shower before we hit the road, but I just couldn't go without. After feeling like I was clean as hell, I hopped out and brushed my teeth. Even though I didn't kiss shit, and damn sure didn't eat any pussy, I felt like my mouth was dirty. I slipped into a Jordan jogger suit, with Jordan brand socks and slide-ins, and then put on my black hat. I grabbed my duffle bag, my keys, and then my phone to make sure Gabriella wasn't on any bullshit, before walking out of the bedroom.

"Okay, let's go, baby," I said and kissed Nina on the corner of her mouth.

Chapter Nine: Nina Joy

We finally got to Santa Barbara, and we were staying at the Four Seasons hotel. It was very upscale and beautiful, but I expected nothing less when traveling with Yazir these days. He always put me up in nice places whenever we went anywhere. He said a woman on my level shouldn't even look a man's way who couldn't give me the world, because I deserved nothing less. You see the type of things he says to me? I was smiling from ear to ear as I thought about it.

"Girl, I need a drink already," Aubrie said as we sat in the lobby.

The boys were checking into the rooms, so we decided to relax. I needed to let my legs stretch from being in the car for so long.

"Yeah, I could use one too, and a damn massage," I chuckled and so did she.

It felt good to be on vacation with my man and best friend. The only thing missing was my boo, Madison.

"So are you two serious or just having fun?" I grinned, referring to Sameer.

"Well, I'm serious as hell, and he better be too," Aubrie poked her lips out and I laughed. I was thinking the exact same thing.

"Have y'all talked about it? Like, is he your boyfriend?" I inquired and she stared off.

"No, we haven't talked about it, but now that you mentioned it, we are gonna do so soon," she raised a brow at me.

"Well, you've been fucking him without a title," I frowned.

"Really, Nina? I recall you giving the panties up to some young fellow on the first date in Vegas," she smiled and I rolled my eyes playfully. I knew she would never let me live that down. I have yet to regret that night, by the way.

"He pulled out all the stops, and before I knew it he was fucking the shit out of me," I giggled and so did she.

Finally, Sameer waved us over, and we all walked to the elevator. We went to our rooms which were next door to each other, and got settled so we could go out and have a few drinks.

"Another fabulous room," I smiled at Yazir. He'd been oddly quiet all night, and I had no idea why. "What's wrong?" I quizzed as I sat in his lap.

"I'm good, why do you ask?" he squinted his eyes.

"Because you're never this quiet," I rubbed his back and kissed his forehead. He seemed to be feeling uneasy about something.

"Oh nah, I'm just tired," he said and moved me out of his lap.

He grabbed his duffle bag, and then went into the bathroom. A few minutes later I heard the shower come on. *Again? He just showered before we left*, I thought. I didn't know what was bothering him, and I was somewhat desperate to find out.

I thought about what that bitch said, and wondered if he had become bored of me already. I quickly got up and took all of my clothes off. I walked into the bathroom naked, and opened the shower door to join him. I was in awe as he stood under the showerhead, letting it drench his sexy body. His beautiful face and beard were dripping water, and his eyes were closed as if he was praying. When I closed the shower door, his eyes popped open.

"You scared me," he half smiled, and ran his hand through his short tapered fro.

"Sorry," I responded and walked to him slowly. I was hoping he was receptive, because that would be embarrassing if he asked me to get out.

Before I could make it to him, he pulled on my arm gently and lifted me up in the air. He brought me down onto his hard dick, and I hugged his neck tightly.

"I love you, Yazir," I whimpered softly. It was like a reflex; I didn't mean to say it yet. I wanted to wait and let him say it first. Fuck!

"I love you more, Nina," he grunted as we continued to make love under the warm water. I was happy to hear that as a response, and so was my body as I exploded on his rod.

After our exotic shower, we both got dressed to have drinks with his brother and Aubrie. Yazir wore white jeans, a white shirt, and all white Jordan Retro 11's. His chain was iced out but subtle, and so was his expensive watch. I loved when he showed his arms, because his tattoos embedded in his pecan complexion were so sexy, and his strong arms always reminded me of how he held me.

I wore a white dress that hugged my body and had thin straps. The top part was similar to a bikini top, and I wore white simple stilettos to match. I parted my hair down the middle, and then added some loose body waves. I put on my red lipstick from MAC, and then put on my locket and favorite watch.

"Oh my gosh, why are you so fucking pretty?" Yazir said, as he looked me up and down while we walked down the hallway of the hotel.

He kissed me lightly so he wouldn't get my lipstick on his own lips, and I slipped my small hand into his secure one. We intertwined our fingers, and then he leaned down and cupped my face with his other hand for another kiss.

"Thank you," I smiled.

We met Aubrie and Sameer at the elevator, and she was wearing a tight red dress. Sameer had on all black, and wore his dreads in a low ponytail. We went to Tydes, and all sat at a table so we could have drinks.

"This place is so peaceful," Aubrie commented as she sipped her drink.

"I know, I can't wait to get a massage here," I said as I glanced around.

"Good thing we're staying a week, because we can get multiple massages," she slapped my hand.

It paid to be dating the owner of Dream Bar and his brother, because taking paid vacations was never a problem.

"I know girl, I can't wait," I said and we all laughed.

"So, has Dasey mentioned Madison?" Aubrie asked. I shook my head while smirking, because Madison would kill her if she were here right now.

"He said she was cute, but I don't think he's ready to stop playing yet," Yazir responded to her and she twisted her lips like she was thinking.

"Why, is she interested?" Sameer looked over at Aubrie.

"Possibly," Aubrie replied and we all laughed out loud.

We had a couple more drinks and an appetizer, before Yazir paid the bill. We waved down a bike taxi, and Yazir and I climbed into the back of one. Sameer and Aubrie decided to go back up to their room with their freaky asses.

The bike rider took us around the city, and it was so cool to watch people having fun, getting drunk, and acting all crazy. In the middle of the ride, Yazir grabbed my hand and kissed the back of it. I glanced over at him quickly, and then diverted my attention back to what was going on outside on the street.

Suddenly, I felt his hands on my waist, and he pulled me over closer to him. I looked up at him, and he mushed his soft full lips against mine repeatedly.

"When I said I loved you earlier, I meant it," he said.

"I know, baby. I meant it too," I caressed his beard and then kissed him again. I loved kissing him. Where did he come from? Maybe Heaven.

He didn't say anything. He just pulled me so close that we were damn near one, and then slid his tongue into my mouth. It tasted sweet because he had just eaten a bag of skittles while were waiting for a bike taxi.

"I can't wait to get you back to the room," he whispered as he kissed me with so much passion, Shakespeare would be in awe at the sight.

I loved this man with everything in me.

Chapter Ten: Aubrie

Back at the room...

I was super tired, but not too tired for some dick and serious conversation. I was also a little tipsy from the three drinks I'd had earlier.

I slipped out of my red dress, and sat Indian style on the bed in just my lace bra and matching underwear. I was thinking about the questions that Nina had asked me earlier, and I felt that conversation was long overdue. I needed a clear understanding of what Sameer and I were doing here. I was not gonna assume shit just for him to throw the *when did I say we were together shit* in my face later on.

"Uh oh, what did I do?" a beautiful smile spread across his sexy mocha face as he stood in the doorway of the bathroom.

He had his dreads hanging down, just the way that I liked them. His shirt was off, showing his abs and pecks, and his dick print was something serious in his sweats.

"Nothing, but come sit down," I patted the bed. He cut the bathroom light off, and then walked over to the bed. He laid down and began kissing on my lower back. "Wait Sam, listen," I chuckled. The feeling of his lips on me made my clit tingle.

"What's up?" he looked up at me.

"What are we doing here?" I questioned.

"We're on vacation, and soon we're gonna be dancing horizontally," he grinned with his fine ass.

"No, stupid," I chuckled. "I mean like, are we- are you-"

"Am I your nigga?" he finished my question for me.

"Yeah, are we boyfriend and girlfriend? Or is this just a having fun type of thing?" I fidgeted as I waited for his answer.

"I thought we were boyfriend and girlfriend, didn't you?" he frowned. I was jumping for joy on the inside right now.

"It seemed like it but I didn't wanna just assume that we were," I shrugged.

"I guess we should've discussed it. But yeah Aubrie, you're mine and I'm yours," he kissed my arm.

He got up and then pushed my shoulder lightly, making me fall backward. He tugged my thong down my legs, and spread them as wide as they would go. He licked his lips as if he was just delivered a gourmet meal. He pushed his boxers to the floor, and his big dick sprang up, making my pussy salivate. He dropped to his knees, and began kissing on my inner thighs.

"Ooohh," I cooed.

He made his way up my thighs to my pussy lips, where he kissed them softly. He took my clit into his mouth, and began sucking it softly. My back arched, and he gripped my waist to bring my pussy further into his mouth.

"Oh, oh my gosh," I cried out as he sucked, slurped, and licked me into a coma damn near. "Saaaam," I whined as he held me in place. I released and he didn't slow up.

I couldn't move as he continued to devour me like it was his last meal. I didn't even have the energy to move my hips in a circular motion because he was sucking everything out of me. He brought his tongue down to my hole, and fucked me with it, making me cum so hard it felt like I was convulsing. He licked me with his tongue a few more times, and then stood up.

"You are definitely mine," I panted as he climbed between my legs and unhooked my bra.

***

It was the next morning, and we had reservations at Bella Vista for the Biltmore brunch. This place was the talk of the town, and we even had to make reservations for it, so I was ready to experience the hype.

I was in Nina's room, and Yazir was in my room with Sameer. "I am starved Nina, hurry up," I chuckled.

"Okay, I'm looking for my shorts," she responded as she walked out of the bathroom in her cute red monokini.

I looked around the room, and I saw the sheets were messed up still. I shook my head at Nina and Yazir's horny asses. She was gonna be pregnant soon at the rate they were going.

"I see y'all had a wild night," I pointed to the bed.

"Something like that," she beamed as she slipped her shorts up her small frame. "I told him I loved him," she said and buttoned her shorts.

"What? And what did he say?" I asked with my mouth open.

"He said he loved me too," she grinned and brushed her long hair.

"Well isn't that cute," I smirked.

I was happy for my friend, because I hated to see her so down while she was with Seth. With Yazir she was herself, and I could see that he made her happy. Sameer said that Nina made Yazir a better person, because now she had him attending church on Sundays with her. I snickered at my thoughts.

"I talked to Sameer last night," I said and leaned on the dresser.

"About being his girl? And what did he say?" She asked with a big ass smile on her face.

"I don't know if I should tell you," I poked my lips out and she frowned.

"Bitch, don't play with me," she folded her arms.

"Aight, he said I am most definitely his girl," I cheesed and she chuckled.

"I know your ass is happy," she said.

"I am," I nodded. Damn, I hadn't felt this giddy about a nigga in I don't know how long.

We were finally ready to go, and Nina decided to go ahead so that nothing would happen to our reservation from being late; especially since this place was a hot commodity.

As I was walking by, I heard voices in my room, so I knew Yazir and Sameer were still in there. I decided to rush them along, so I walked closer while shaking my head at them. I stopped myself from slipping my key into the door when I heard their tones. They sounded like they were discussing something secretive, and I was a nosey ass person. *Please don't let Sameer be hiding some shit, at least not right now Lord.* I silently prayed as I put my ear to the door.

"Wait, so you fucked Gabriella and Kiara yesterday?" Sameer asked Yazir and my stomach dropped.

"Yes, nigga. I was not planning that shit. I went over there to shut her ass down, and I don't know what the fuck happened," Yazir replied in a frustrated tone.

"You gon' tell her?" Sameer asked.

"For what?" Yazir quizzed and I could tell he was frowning. "So she can leave me? No, I ain't saying shit. I'm just gonna sweep it under the rug. Ain't like it's gonna happen again," he explained.

I shoved my keycard into the door, and then walked in. This nigga had me hotter than a summer day in California. I wanted to just charge Yazir as soon as I saw him sitting down in the room.

"Hey baby, are y'all ready?" Sameer questioned and gave me a toothless smile. I could tell he was wondering if I'd heard anything.

"Yeah, Nina has already, umm, headed over to make sure our reservation doesn't get lost," I half smiled although fuming.

"Alright, come on," Sameer tapped Yazir's chest and he got up.

We all walked out, and I stayed behind a little. I grabbed Yazir's arm lightly, and he turned to look down at me.

"If you don't tell her I will," was all I said before jogging to catch up to Sameer.

I looked back over my shoulder after locking arms with my man, and Yazir was looking like his dog died. I didn't care though; he was the one who messed up.

When we walked into the breakfast spot, Nina waved us over to the table she'd been seated at. When we neared it, she got up and kissed all over Yazir's face. I hated to see her so happy now, because she was gonna get her heart broken very soon.

It seemed like whenever my best friend tried to find love, something went wrong. First it was Phillip dying, then Seth being a controlling asshole, and now this nigga cheating on her. I clenched my jaw as I reminisced.

"Chill out, babe," Yazir chuckled nervously, before sitting down next to her. Her smile was so wide, and it broke my heart.

"They have unlimited mimosas, and I'm gonna take full advantage," she cheesed and I gave her a half smile back.

Yazir leaned over to kiss her neck, and I shot daggers at him. He cleared his throat, and then picked up the menu to look over it. I did the same before we finally ordered our food.

If he didn't tell her before the day was over, I would. I'll be damned if I allow my friend to be out here looking stupid.

Chapter Ten: Yazir

What I was feeling right now was unexplainable. I hadn't planned on revealing what I'd done to Nina, but now I had to. Either she could hear it from me, or from her best friend, and the latter would be ten times worse.

I wished I could go back in time, because I could've went about the situation differently. When that bitch told me to give her a second, I should've said no, and then threatened her right then and there. But no, being the dumb ass that I am, I fell for her pussy trap. Now I'm here sweating like a nigga on death row, because I have to tell Nina that I cheated on her with a bitch that I just said didn't matter to me. I have to tell her that although I loved her, I temporarily didn't care about her feelings because fixing my hard dick seemed to be more important. I just hoped that she could forgive me, and I hoped she didn't run back to that bitch ass nigga, Seth.

"Are you ready to go shopping?" Nina came from the balcony smiling. She had the most beautiful smile ever, and I was scared that it might be the last time I got to see it.

We'd just come from brunch a couple hours ago, and now we were gonna go sightseeing and shopping. Why couldn't Aubrie just let me have this vacation with Nina, and tell her when we got back in town? Why did she have to know now? What if this is the last time I get to spend with her? Shouldn't I be able to savor the moment?

I sat up and wiped my eyes before exhaling heavily.

"Are you tired?" She walked over to me and sat down. She kissed my face and rubbed my head.

"No, I'm okay, baby," I sighed.

She was wearing shorts and a red tube top that had her whole stomach out. Her hair was in one long braid, and she smelled like carrot cake. I knew she wore that scented body butter for me, and it made me feel even worse. I was gonna miss that smell.

I looked to my right at her, and just admired how pretty she was. "Are you okay?" she asked sweetly as she continued to rub my head.

I pecked her full lips, and then next thing I knew we were kissing hungrily. I leaned her back, and began to pull on her shorts. I stopped abruptly, and then sat up and dropped my head into my hands.

"Yaz, what's wrong?" she asked and sat up. *Just get the shit out,* I told myself.

"Baby, remember when I said that I wasn't perfect?" I quizzed and she nodded slowly.

"Nobody is-"

"Nina, just listen for a second," I cut her off and she shook her head to say okay. "Uh, and remember when you said you would stick by me?" I inquired. She paused then nodded again, but a single tear slipped out of her eye. "Why are you crying?" I questioned and thumbed the tear away.

"Finish what you were gonna say," she replied.

I stared into her eyes, and my heart started to beat fast. I knew she knew, and she was just waiting for me to say it. I could see how disappointed she was. I could hear her telling herself that she was right about me all along. I so badly wanted to backpedal but I couldn't.

"I slept with someone else yesterday evening. That's why I was late coming home to leave to Santa Barbara," I finally got it out, and then swallowed the lump in my throat.

"Who was it?" she asked as more tears raced down her cheeks.

She sniffled a little, and let the tears flow. I reached to wipe them but she moved her face away. She wouldn't even let me touch her, and I started to feel queasy.

"Nina-"

"Was it the girl from the club?" she inquired. I opened my mouth but nothing came out. "I thought so," she responded calmly and stood up.

I got up to follow her, but she slammed the bathroom door in my face. A few moments passed, and I could hear her crying without sound. You know, when no sound is coming out, but their breathing pattern tells you how hurt they are. My eyes watered as I listened to her sob. Finally, noise came out, and she was weeping hard as fuck.

I twisted the knob but it was locked. "Nina," I beat on the door and twisted the knob again.

She didn't say anything; all she did was cry. She was crying so hard it sounded physically painful.

"Nina, baby, open the door, please," I begged. She turned on the running water to drown out the sound of her sobbing. I walked out of the room, and banged on my brother's door. Aubrie answered it and rolled her eyes. "Aubrie, can you help me get your friend out of the bathroom," I said defeated.

"Why, what happened?" She bucked her eyes.

"I told her and she locked herself in the bathroom," I replied.

Before I could finish, Aubrie ran past me to my room. I followed after her, and she knocked on the bathroom door after I unlocked the hotel room.

"Nina, it's me," she said and twisted the knob like I had done prior. A few moments later, the door opened slightly for Aubrie to come in. I tried to as well, but Aubrie stopped me. "Just leave for a little bit, Yazir," she put her hand up.

"What? No! Let me talk to her," I frowned.

What the fuck was she trying to do? I wasn't about to leave her in there crying like that. I felt like the longer I let her stay in there away from me, the harder it would be to return to her good graces.

"You can, but let me calm her down first," she pleaded.

"Close the fucking door!" Nina yelled through tears.

"Baby, let me talk to you!" I yelled back, but Aubrie slammed the door in my face and locked it. I snatched the lamp off of the nightstand and ripped it out of the wall. I stormed out of the room but then went back in. "Nina!" I screamed and beat on the door.

I got no response, so I continued knocking. I couldn't take it anymore so I busted the door down. It flew open, and was only hanging on by one of the hinges. Having to pay for these hotel damages was the least of my fucking worries.

"Really Yazir?" Aubrie frowned at me but I ignored her ass. Nina was sitting on the floor and her face was drenched in tears.

"Baby, I'm sorry, it was a mistake, I-" I kneeled down by her.

"I don't care! I don't wanna be with you anymore! You don't love me you fucking liar!" She sobbed violently and yelled so loud my ears rang.

The words that had just escaped her lips had so much passion behind them that it was scary. I could tell she meant every word. I kissed her full wet lips gently and repeatedly, as she cried like a newborn. I didn't know what the fuck to do right now. I was so inexperienced in this department.

"I'm sorry, Nina, it won't happen again, baby. I love you so much, you have to believe me," I whispered as I kissed her lips. I didn't care if she didn't reciprocate.

Aubrie walked out of the bathroom and the room. I could see she was irritated that I wouldn't give Nina some space but I just couldn't.

I stood Nina up, and hugged her tightly. I was hugging her as if I thought she might run away and never come back.

"Why Yazir?" she wept into my shirt.

Her body jerked because she was crying so hard. I didn't respond to her question, because I had no reason other than I was horny and there was pussy in my face.

Getting lost in my thoughts, my grip loosened unbeknownst to me, and she suddenly snatched away from me, and then rushed out of the hotel room and down the hall. She hopped on the elevator, and it closed before I could get on. I waited for it to come back, and then rode it down to the lobby impatiently. Once I stepped off, I looked around frantically for her but I didn't see her.

"Excuse me, did you see a girl wearing shorts and a red top come down here?" I asked the clerk and she shook her head no. I rushed outside and I didn't see her there either. "Fuck!" I hollered in the parking lot, before grabbing ahold of my hair.

Chapter Ten: Sameer

Hearing Yazir admit to Nina his infidelity, and the way she reacted only made me want to keep my secret from Aubrie even longer. Cherelle would be home soon though, so I knew I had to come clean sooner or later.

I had no idea how Aubrie would react, but I don't think anything could be worse than the way Nina reacted. Shit, maybe Aubrie wouldn't be mad at all. I didn't cheat or anything, I just have a little wife that I'm not emotionally married to.

"I hate to see my friend like this." Aubrie came out of the bathroom and sat on the bed.

"She was pretty broken up, huh?" I raised a brow and she nodded her head yes.

I'd heard Nina crying from in here. She sounded like someone had died or some shit. She had me ready to whoop my brother's ass for breaking her up like that. If she had me feeling bad, I could only imagine how he felt.

"I don't understand some niggas. It's like they claim they're so into you, and then they do shit like this," she scoffed.

"Sometimes people make mistakes, Brie," I sat next to her.

"But it's dumb. Yazir was all over Nina, acting like he had found the woman of his dreams, and when he gets her he cheats. What kind of sense does that make?" she frowned. "He should've just left her alone," she sighed.

"Yeah, it wasn't a smart move on his part, but hopefully they can work it out," I said, kind of trying to see her opinion. I wanted to see if she was a fan of forgiveness like I hoped.

"I don't know if she should try. She deserves better than that. Nina is a good woman, and she shouldn't have to settle for Yazir," she turned her lip up while shaking her head.

"Settle? You think she's settling? I think she loves my brother," I frowned.

"I know she does, but what I mean is she shouldn't have to be with a man who will be unfaithful to her."

"You can't just leave a relationship whenever you hit a bump in the road, Aubrie. If it's worth it you should try and work it out," I explained.

"Understandable, but what I'm saying is I don't think it's worth it."

"I thought you said she seemed so much happier with him and all this other shit," I furrowed my brows.

"She did but, they haven't even been together that long, and his age and immaturity is already showing," she rolled her neck.

"Immaturity? Men of all ages cheat. I know niggas in their sixties that stick their dick in other bitches all the time," I turned my lip up. She was irritating me with her stupid ass conclusions and assumptions.

"Well, maybe they just never grew up. All I know is that if my man cheats or lies to me, I don't care if we're twenty-five or eighty, I'm gone," she bucked her eyes.

"I hear you," I exhaled.

How could I tell her when she had this attitude? She pretty much just told me she would leave me if I told her about Cherelle. I needed to find a way to tell her without it sounding like some cheating shit. I mean I *wasn't* cheating.

Cherelle was my wife on paper, but definitely not my wife in my heart. I needed to get Aubrie out of her guarded mentality before I could tell her anything. Right now she was in defense mode, and I couldn't tell her shit. As soon as the word wife spilled off of my lips, she would go berserk. Why did shit have to be so complicated?

"I'm gonna go check on her," she said and then stood up.

I stood up as well, and then grabbed her arm. I pulled her close, and then kissed her lips gently. She half smiled, and then threw her arms around my neck. Our tongues wrestled, and I reached under her to lift her dress up. Once it was off, I unhooked her bra, and then devoured her nipples.

"Sameeeer," she purred.

I pushed her back onto the bed, and then began to undress. I wasn't sure how much longer she would be mine, so I wanted to take full advantage right now.

Once I was naked, I pulled her panties down and off, and then flipped her onto all fours. I spread her legs with my knees, and then positioned my dick at her opening.

"Uuuh, aaahh," she cooed as I slowly started to plunge in and out of her. She was starting to adjust to my size, so I sped up a little. "Sameer, shit baby," she sucked on her bottom lip and gripped the sheets. The side of her face was buried into the pillow as I banged her out.

"Fuck, babe," I grunted and gripped her small waist.

She played with her nipples as I applied pressure to her asshole with my thumb. She was so wet I could feel it dripping down her legs.

WHAM!

I smacked her smooth round ass, and the sight of it jiggling made my dick harder. “I'm about to fucking nut already,” I groaned.

“I'm gonna cum again babe, aaah, aahhh,” she called out in a high pitched voice, and then bit the pillow with her perfect teeth.

I leaned down to kiss the side of her lips softly, while going ham from behind, and soon after we exploded. We collapsed down, and I groped her body as we laid there kissing.

“You know you're mine forever,” I whispered. She nodded and slipped her tongue back into my mouth.

What the fuck was I gonna do?

Chapter Eleven: Nina Joy

I'd been sitting on the beach for the last four hours, crying non-stop. I was embarrassed and I felt like a fool. I'd been floating around California like I had prince on my arm, when he was nothing more than a typical nigga. I left someone who had loved me, for a man who couldn't make it three months before cheating on me. Seth may not have loved me in the way that I preferred, but he did love me. I was nothing more than a cheap thrill to Yazir, and that's what hurt the most.

I should've followed my first mind, and never even given him the time of the day. Instead, I wanted to be stupid and let him sweep me off of my feet. I was so wrapped up in our love affair, that I only thought with my heart and not my mind. Now, here I was looking just like the many bitches he had dated before. I guess that girl was right when she said Yazir moved on quickly.

He acted as if he was so into me, and had finally found the one, when all along I was no different than any other woman. If I were different, he would've treated me as such. If I were different, his feelings for me would've stopped him from sticking his dick in a girl that he'd just told me meant nothing to him. She's probably at home laughing at me, and how I fell for his impeccable charm.

I don't even understand what his point was in entering a relationship with me. I mean he fucked me on the first night, he should've just moved on. I should've just went back to Seth and married him like I had intended to. Yeah, Seth wasn't the greatest, but with my luck he was the best thing I had. Now he probably had no interest in being with me. I'm sure he saw me as a foolish girl who makes rash decisions. I fell for oldest trick in the book, and Yazir didn't even have to try that hard.

Tears made their way down my cheeks in abundance, as I thought about what got me here on this beach. Why did he have to do this? And I stupidly just confessed my love for him. He had the nerve to tell me he loved me too, when he had just slept with that whore. No wonder he was living in the fucking shower.

"Are you okay?" some white girl asked as she walked by with her boyfriend.

"Yes, I'm fine," I smiled up at her, and discreetly wiped my cheeks.

"Okay," she smiled back.

I moved to a more secluded area, and watched the ocean for a couple more hours to clear my head. My face was in pain from crying, and my chest was sore from it heaving up and down with such velocity.

It was dark by now, and I had no money or phone because I left it all in the room. I hailed a taxi back to the hotel, and then asked the taxi driver to wait for me. I promised I would pay him, and thankfully he agreed. When I entered the hotel, I went straight to the front desk for a key. I scoped out my surroundings first, because I didn't want Yazir running up on me. But knowing his lying ass, he probably already had some new bitch on his arm.

"Oh, Mr. Willis has been looking for you all night ma'am," the clerk said after I explained to her who I was.

"Is he in the room?" I asked. I didn't want to go in there if he was.

One reason was because I wouldn't be able to deal if I saw him with some hoe, and secondly because I didn't want him trying to hold me captive to plead his case.

"No, he just left again to go look for you on the beach," she replied and gave me a sympathetic expression. I could tell she felt bad for him; if only she knew the reasoning behind my antics.

"Thanks," I said and took the key from her.

I rushed up to the room, and when I got there, I grabbed as many things as I could. I saw the room looked a mess, and remembered he'd been acting out before knocking the bathroom door down.

I rushed back down, and got a taxi to a different hotel. I didn't wanna go home yet, because my only home was with my mother, and she would go in on me if she saw me sleeping there. I didn't feel like hearing her *I told you so* speech, nor did I wanna hear her tell me to go make amends with Seth.

Once I got to my new room, I cut all the lights off, sunk under the covers, and cried myself to sleep. I wanted to be at peace, and sleep was the only way I could get some at the moment.

***

I woke up the next morning with a horrible headache, but decided I would not spend the rest of my vacation crying. Fuck Yazir and his lying cheating ass. And fuck Seth's controlling ass too! I was gonna enjoy this time off of work, and away from my regular life.

I got up to take a quick shower and brush my teeth, because I wanted to lay out on the beach today. I had a new thong bathing suit, and I wanted to show it off, especially now that I was single.

I slipped into my skimpy suit, and then put my long hair into a big bun on my head. I smoothed sunscreen all over my smooth chocolate complexion, and then put on my flip-flops. When I grabbed my phone, wristlet, and room keycard, I saw Yazir and Aubrie had been blowing me up.

Me: *I'm fine. Don't tell Yazir anything. Enjoy your trip with Sameer and I will talk to you when I get back.* I texted to Aubrie. She texted back asking me where I was, but I ignored it. I needed time to myself.

I walked out to the beach, and enjoyed all the adoring looks I got. I laid my towel down, and then laid back on it to watch the water. It was so peaceful seeing the water move about, and watching the kids play in it. I smiled at the families spending time together, and wondered if I would ever have a family of my own.

As I got lost in the sound of the ocean, and watching people enjoy themselves, I heard my phone ringing. It was dumb ass Yazir again, blowing me up. What the fuck did he think calling me constantly was gonna do?

I silenced my phone, and then went back to watching the water. After a couple hours, I picked up my towel and then went to have a drink at one of the surrounding bars. This trip was gonna be a blast, single and all.

Chapter Eleven: Yazir

The next evening...

I had no idea where Nina was, and I was going crazy. Was she still in Santa Barbara? And if she was, where was she? If she wasn't here, I hoped she wasn't laid up with her ex.

I looked in my recent call list and saw I had called her thirty damn times. I had text her just as much, and she hadn't responded to anything. I hated this shit right now, and I was miserable.

I'd never been this bothered by any woman. She had me losing sleep because I couldn't stop thinking about her. I felt like I was missing a vital organ or some shit. I just felt sick as hell. A part of me wanted to hate Aubrie, because I felt like this was her fault. But when I came to my senses, I knew I was to blame.

I had no idea if Nina would come back to me, but I was gonna try and convince her to. I had never been in a relationship where I had to fight for my woman, so I had no idea where to start. Was I supposed to buy her something? Send her flowers? Give her space? What if giving her space made her get over me? Or what if smothering her only worsened things? I didn't fucking know.

I was used to getting what I wanted, who I wanted, and when I wanted it. Not being able to snap my fingers and have Nina in my arms again was new to me. Women have always been the least of my worries, and this was first time one had been at the top of my worry list.

I even tried to convince myself that she meant nothing to me, and that I'd only been with her for a short time, but that shit didn't work. Nina showed me things that no other woman had, and I knew I couldn't find that just anywhere. She talked to me, joked with me, and was interested in my life. Most chicks just wanted to be in my presence because of my status and money; they couldn't care less about why I was angry or sad. When I was sick, she would cook soup for me and shit, give me massages until I fell asleep; it's just so many things I could name. She made me enjoy my life a bit more. I loved that girl, and I knew she was one of a kind. Just the thought of me never being able to be with her again made my throat jump.

I looked at my phone again to see if she had replied to any of my text messages, even though I knew she hadn't. I just wanted to go back to the many nights we stayed up talking and fucking, but I knew that shit was over. I wish I had have known then that she would only be in my life a short time, because I would've cherished our days together.

It was 6pm, and Aubrie and Sameer were gonna go out to a club. Aubrie seemed okay with the fact that her best friend was somewhat missing now. Before, she was just as frantic, but now her attitude had shifted. Something told me she'd been in contact with Nina, but I knew she would never tell me. I couldn't blame her though, because that's where her loyalty lied.

I put on my Jordan slide-ins, and grabbed my wallet and keys. I had on black sweats and a matching black Jordan sweater. I wasn't in the mood to look fly or be on vacation at all. I just wanted to take some Hennessy to the head, and figure out how to get my baby back.

I walked until I made it to the beach, and I saw there weren't many people on it. Everyone was walking to the club, to dinner, or getting ready to. As I was walking along the sand, my breath got caught in my throat when I spotted Nina lying on a towel. She had on a tan bathing suit, showing off her perfect body. She was lying on her flat stomach, and I could see her bottoms were a thong. Seeing her right now was so surreal for some reason. It seemed like I was gonna wake up any minute.

I walked closer but slowly, because I felt if she saw me she would run off. Her eyes were closed, and she appeared to be napping. I sat down next to her very gently, because again, I didn't want her waking up and running off. She smelled so good, and she looked so beautiful sleeping there. I missed her ass. She had a nigga feeling sappy as shit.

I placed my hand on her small back, and kissed down her spine softly. She stirred a little, so I kissed further down her back. I yearned for her. She jumped and then turned on her back.

"What are you doing?" she frowned slightly and wiped her eyes.

"I missed you, baby," I started to kiss on her neck. She tried to move, but I grabbed her body closer to me. She was not getting away like before.

"Move, Yazir." I could hear her crying as she pushed my chest.

"Baby, I'm sorry, don't do me like this," I said in a low tone, as I groped her little body with my big hands. I could feel her giving in. I had to have her; there was no way I could let her move on from me. "I'm sorry, Nina," I pleaded. She just cried as I kissed on her lips, neck, and shoulders.

"Get off me!" she sobbed and pushed me with all her might. I was way stronger than her, so I didn't budge. I gripped her torso tighter, and started to suck on her full lips.

WHAM!

She slapped the shit out of me. "I said get off me!" she sniffled and then got up. She grabbed her little skirt thing, and wrapped her bottom half in it before running off.

Chapter Eleven: Aubrie

Back at the hotel...

Now that I knew Nina was okay, I could somewhat enjoy the rest of my trip here. Sameer and I were going out to eat and to this little club in the city. I was excited because this trip had been drama filled for the past day and a half, and it was finally starting to feel like a vacation again. I loved Nina, but I wanted to be drama free for one night at least.

"You ready, sexy?" Sameer asked me. I brushed my edges down, and then grabbed the little clutch that I was wearing out tonight. I walked by Sameer, and he shook his head as he took in my appearance. "So sexy," he commented and then opened the hotel door for me.

I was wearing a simple white dress that was strapless and short. I wore white sandal heels to match, and my hair was in a low side ponytail.

We headed to this restaurant named Wine Cask. It was an upscale restaurant that specialized in all kinds of wine. There was nothing more relaxing than a glass of wine, so I was anxious to get there.

"Don't get too drunk," Sameer taunted as we sat down at the table.

"I will do my best," I grinned and he smirked. We placed our order with the waitress, ordering two bottles of wine so we could go in. "This is so nice, baby," I cheesed and he kissed the back of my hand.

"I know. It feels good to travel with you," he bit his lip and squinted his eyes. He had on a black button up, and his dreads were hanging loosely. I loved when he wore them down, because they framed his sexy mocha face perfectly.

"We should do this more often then," I winked.

"And where would you like to go?" he inquired.

"Somewhere pretty like Paris, or Italy or-" the sound of his phone buzzing loudly cut me off.

"Give me like two seconds baby," he hopped up and rushed off.

Okay now I was pissed. It wasn't even the usual time; this was way later than usual. I sat there with my arms folded, and bounced my leg repeatedly as I waited for him to come back.

"Fuck this!" I said and got up from the table.

I rushed over to the exit, and waved one of those bike taxis down. I quickly climbed on, and directed him back to the hotel. Sameer had me fucked up if he thought he was just gonna be answering calls during our dinner. If he couldn't take time out of his *work* to fully give me his attention, I didn't want his ass anyway.

By the time I reached the hotel, my phone was going off because Sameer was calling me. I dropped it back into my clutch, and then went back up to the room. I pulled my shoes off, and then went into my bag to get my makeup wipes. After taking my make up off, I needed a hot bath.

As I was running some bath water, I heard the door open and close. I could hear him storming to the bathroom, but I declined to look his way.

"So you just leave and don't say shit?" he barked. I stood up once the water was hot enough, and then grabbed some towels off of the shelf. He started chuckling at the fact that I was ignoring him. "Aubrie," he said. I didn't say anything, and took a capful of my body wash to the faucet so that I could make bubbles. "Alright, I'm sorry but I had to take that call," he touched the small of my back. I was still silent, so he took the capful of bubble bath out of my hands, and tossed it to the floor before turning me to face him. “Baby, it was just business,” he grinned like something was funny.

“If you expect me to believe that, you're really gonna piss me off,” I spat and moved his hands off of me. I walked around him so that I could get a nightgown from my bag.

“Aubrie, really? What you want? Some sucker ass nigga who spends all his time in your face? Those niggas are broke!” he shouted as I grabbed my undergarments and nightgown from my bag.

“Well, at least a broke nigga can pay attention to his girl,” I said and walked past him to the bathroom.

“Man, stop being so fucking bitter!” he shouted. Oh, he was really trying me tonight!

“Bitter?” I dropped everything in my hand. “I'm bitter because I'm tired of you running off and answering business calls? Why is it that these business calls have to be answered in private, huh? Every other business call is answered right in front of me!” I screamed.

“So what! You're so scared that somebody is trying to play you that you can't even fucking chill!” he hollered.

“You want me to chill so you can pull the wool over my eyes, but that-”

“I know it ain't gon' happen!” he imitated me and did air quotes. “You gon' be alone forever thinking like that, baby.” He shook his head and plopped down on the bed.

“That's perfectly fine. I'd rather be alone than be with some fake ass, lying ass nigga for the rest of my life,” I folded my arms. He shook his head at me and laughed.

“Come here,” he said and I looked away from him. “Get your mean ass over here,” he chuckled. I blew out hot air, and then made my way over to him. He gripped my waist, and then looked up into my eyes since he was sitting on the bed. "Can you please come back out with me? I will turn my phone off," he said. He was so fucking sexy. He licked his lips as he waited for my answer.

"I'm not hungry anymore," I frowned.

"Well I am, so can I get in your bath?" He bit his lip.

"I guess," I shot him a half smile. He stood up and towered over me. I turned around and then looked over my shoulder at him.

"Fuck," he licked his lips again, and stroked his beard before following me into the bathroom.

I was gonna stop tripping on him until I got some stronger proof. I would be mad as hell if he stopped fucking with me over my paranoia. So from now on, I was gonna chill until further notice and enjoy my time with my man.

Chapter Twelve: Nina Joy

The Santa Barbara trip had ended, and although I didn't wanna see Yazir after he snuck up on me at the beach, Aubrie convinced me to ride home with she and Sameer. Yazir tried to get me into the car with him, but I wasn't having it.

I was putting on some chai colored lipstick in the back room before starting my shift. I was trying to stay afloat, but this fake happy shit was not working. On top of everything else, I had stomach cramps and I was depressed, so I did not feel like making drinks, or dealing with these fake ass rich niggas trying to boss up in VIP.

As I was about to put my gloss away, I heard the back room door open and then lock. I booked it towards the door, and I saw Yazir standing in front of it. He looked good wearing jeans, Nikes, a snapback, and a heather gray colored crew neck. I rolled my eyes and then walked back to my locker to put my gloss up. When I turned around he was right in my face, and his cologne hit me like a ton of bricks.

"I'm gonna be late," I said. He placed his hand against the locker, and leaned down in my face.

"So you're never gonna talk to me?" he asked and nibbled on his full bottom lip with his perfect teeth. Why was he so gorgeous?

"Talk about what? You cheated on me, and now it's over," I shrugged like I didn't have a care in the world. I wanted him to believe I didn't care anymore.

"And that's it? You don't wanna give me another chance, Nina?" he frowned as if he was so fucking confused.

"No, I don't," I folded my arms and cocked my head.

"So when you said you loved me what did that mean?" He cocked his head, imitating me, and then squinted his eyes. He was sooooo good looking, why Lord?

"I loved you before you broke my heart. I loved who I thought you were," I responded and quickly wiped the one tear that had cascaded down my cheek. Fuck, so much for my nonchalant facade.

"So, you let that nigga hit you, and you took him back, but the nigga you love gets no chances. Makes sense," he nodded.

"I knew I should've never told you what Seth did. You're disgusting." I shook my head and tried to move past him. He grabbed my shoulders and put me up against the lockers.

"Nina, you're driving me crazy! I'm sorry, baby, it was a mistake and I don't know what you want me to do!" he shouted. I could see in his eyes that he was defeated. I started to feel for him until I remembered he was the one who hurt me.

"I want you to leave me alone, Yazir! It's over and it's never gonna happen between us again!" I glared up at him. "If you really felt so strongly about me, you would've been faithful and we would still be together."

He tried to kiss me but I moved my face away. He sighed and then turned around to leave the back room. Finally.

I worked my shift and I tried to keep myself from crying. I couldn't get Yazir off of my mind. I messed up about seven drinks tonight because I couldn't concentrate, and my manager was pissed at me. He had to give out a lot of free drink vouchers on my behalf, and my tips were slim to none.

When the clock read 3am, I was ecstatic. I drove to my mother's house since that's where I'd been staying since I got back from Santa

Barbara. I was looking for an apartment, and I had recently found one, but I couldn't move in until a week from now.

As soon as I got home, I went straight to the shower. I cleaned myself, brushed my teeth, and then climbed into bed to watch the *Facts of Life*. A couple hours later, I drifted off to sleep, unintentionally dreaming of Yazir.

***

I woke up and there was a bouquet of roses on my nightstand. I sat up and my mom was standing in the doorway shaking her head.

"That little boy had them delivered," she scoffed. "I told you it wasn't gonna last Nina, and now look at you. You're back at square one. You need to go and make up with Seth," she sighed.

"I don't want to be with Seth," I pinned my hair up.

"You wanna be with that kid, don't you?" she squinted her eyes.

"First off stop calling him that, his name is Yazir. Secondly, I don't want him either," I shook my head and she left.

I hopped up and closed the door behind her, and then locked it in case she attempted to return. I went back to the roses, and retrieved the note that was tucked in them. It was a letter, so I quickly unfolded it.

Nina,

Baby, I don't know what to say or do to convince you to come back to me but I'm dying. I never knew I could feel this way about anyone until I met you. I will do anything you need me to do in order for there to be an 'us' again. I can't even get a good night's sleep because I miss you so much. I think about you all day to the point where I can't even focus. I even almost hit a damn pedestrian, because my mind was so consumed with thoughts of your pretty smile, and all the good times we had together. Nina, despite what you may think or believe, I LOVE YOU SO MUCH. Even if you don't love me, just know I love you more than anything. No one will ever compare to you, and you're the best thing that has ever happened to me. You got me acting out of character like a muthafucka. I've never written a love letter in my life. Then again, you don't answer any of my calls, texts, or Instagram DMs, so this was the only other form of communication I could think of. If I have to get on my knees and beg you to be my baby again, just say the word and I will do it. I promise I will never hurt you again. Not just because I'm so in love with you, but also because I never wanna be the reason you cry that hard again. Hearing how much I hurt you, and seeing it in the way you sat on that bathroom floor nearly snapped a nigga's heart in two. Please give us another chance, baby. I just wanna be able to lie naked with you, and talk until the sun comes up like we always do. I miss your scent, your laugh, and your sparkling personality. I feel like a monster for what I did to you, and I hope you can read the sincerity in my words, baby girl. Just think about it. I love you Nina Joy Jeffries.

A tear fell from my eye onto the paper, and then I quickly folded it up. My heart was saying to allow him back into my life, but my pride wouldn't allow me to. Yazir had me so open, and then he just crushed me. He crushed me for no reason at all.

I stuffed the note into my wallet, and then I went to shower. Once out, I spread Yazir's favorite scent all over my damp body, and then got dressed because Aubrie, Madison, and I were gonna have breakfast together.

When I walked outside, Seth was standing there with chocolates, a teddy bear, and a big grin on his face.

"Good morning," I said, a little freaked out.

"Good morning, sweetheart. You look beautiful," he replied.

"Thanks Seth," I sighed and walked down my mother's porch steps.

"I was wondering if you'd be willing to go to dinner with me, Nina," he stared into my eyes sincerely.

"Seth-"

"Please, I'm not the same guy, Nina. Not having you with me gave me time to think about the way I've been treating you," he handed me the chocolates and teddy bear. I heard the door open, and I turned around to see my mom smiling in the doorway.

"Just one date, and we can go from there," he said. I looked into his beautiful eyes, and gave him a half smile.

"Fine, just one date," I agreed. He grabbed me into a hug, and kissed the corner of my mouth.

"I have to go," I said as I pulled away and then rushed off to my car.

Chapter Twelve: Yazir

I woke up in my den, with a bag of Skittles next to my head, and still holding a bottle of whiskey. All I had on were boxers, socks, and an open robe. My phone was ringing off the hook, and I scrambled to my feet thinking it was Nina. *The letter must've done it*, I thought. When I picked my phone up I saw it was my mother, and I felt bad for being disappointed.

"Hey Ma, what's up?" I slurred before taking another sip of my whiskey. My head was throbbing but I didn't care.

"Honey, can you do me a favor?" she asked.

"Anything for you," I replied and leaned my head back.

"Please give Matthew his job back, baby. He's broke as hell. My sister has been trying to reach him, but his phone is cut off. We're worried about him," she pleaded.

"Ma, I tried to help Matt, but he doesn't wanna be helped, aight? I gave him a job, and when he had money he wasn't even sending any down there to his kids and woman," I frowned and tried to stand up, but I was too tipsy so I fell back down.

"I know he's a fuck up baby, but he's your cousin. Do it for your aunt Stella, Robyn, and his children. Take a portion of his check and send it down or something, but he needs to get back on his feet," she said.

"Alright Ma, I will see what I can do," I replied.

"Thank you baby, and thank you for the purse and shoes too. How is your girlfriend doing? I can't wait to meet her!" she beamed. The mention of Nina made my chest ache.

"I don't have a girlfriend anymore, Ma." I sipped out of my bottle again.

"What did you do, Yaz?" I could hear her frowning.

"Why do assume it was me?" I scooted to the edge of the couch.

"Because I know you," she chuckled. "Now spill."

"I cheated on her, Ma," I sighed. I felt like trash every time I thought about it. I knew Nina deserved better than that.

"How did that happen, Yazir? You were talking to me like you found the one," my mom replied. I could tell she was slightly upset with me.

"I know and I did. I just had a moment of weakness. But she's washed her hands of me completely," I shrugged and shook my head.

"Well, I guess you will learn for the next relationship," my mom exhaled. I didn't want another relationship; I wanted Nina Joy Jeffries.

"Thanks, but I'm gonna holla at your nephew, and I will call you tomorrow," I said, not wanting to talk about Nina anymore.

"Okay, bye, honey. I love you."

"I love you too."

I got up so I could wash my ass and brush my teeth. I felt a little sick because of all the whiskey I'd drank on a somewhat empty stomach, so Ms. Brenda made me some oatmeal and a glass of papaya juice. I still had the latest bottle that Nina bought me. *You gotta stop thinking about her man*, I told myself.

I'd made a habit of checking her Instagram every morning. All I saw were pictures of her having fun with her friends, and living life, or in my mind- being okay without me. She never posted any cryptic messages to let me know she missed me or anything. She was smiling in damn near every picture, and although beautiful, I hated to see it if I wasn't in person to enjoy it.

Once I was clean, dressed, and fed, I drove over to Matthew's condo. I was against employing him again, but I wanted to put my mom and Aunt Stella at ease. I knew my aunt was probably about to pass out at the thought of her son being in Los Angeles with no money.

My family down South saw California as this fast paced town, with gang bangers and celebrities everywhere. In some areas it was like that, but not on every damn corner like they thought.

I hopped out and beat on the door, until Hell came and answered it in some shorts that were all up in her crotch, and a bathing suit top. If you put an AK to my head, I still wouldn't sniff the crotch of those shorts. I knew they were rancid.

She rolled her eyes at me and then called my cousin. He came down the stairs, and then stopped in his tracks when he saw me.

"Let me talk to you, Matt," I said and walked to his living room.

I sat down and he entered the room a few moments later. Hell was right on his heels, and when she reached the La-Z-Boy, she plopped down. The smell of flaming hot garbage immediately permeated the air. Was Matthew's nose broken? How could he lay down with that? She'd come home to one of those damn police water hose spraying her in the face if it was me.

"Look, I'm willing to put you to work, only because you're my cousin," I said.

"Damn man, I appreciate-"

"You won't have your same position as a manager of the smoke shop though. You can work security of the Blue Dream corporate building," I cut in.

"Nigga, what! I'm your fucking cousin! The fuck I look like being security! I need my old position," he grimaced.

This nigga was acting like I needed him. This was a favor, and from the looks of him, Hell, and this condo, he needed anything he could get.

"That ain't available. Security is all I got for you, so take it or leave it," I stared him in the eyes.

"I'm leaving it," he stood his ground. I nodded and stood to my feet. He wasn't in a position to be picky. "Let me know if you change your mind," I said before turning to leave.

"That's really fucked up, Yazir! And you know it!" he screamed after me once he realized I was not gonna fold for him. I ignored him as I walked to the door. "It's cool though, because when I come up you ain't getting shit!" he added.

"Hopefully, you give some to your kids and girlfriend," was all I said before leaving.

This nigga was lazy as hell, and there was no way he would ever make anything of himself at this rate. But shit, if he did somehow get his shit together and come up, I would actually be happy for him. At the end of the day he was my cousin, and I liked to see my family and friends succeed. I was never a hater.

I got in my car, and I was tempted to call Nina. She could always make me feel better, but I knew she wouldn't answer. I didn't know why I was so attached to her, and I hadn't even known her that long. I guess she made a hell of an impression on me, and with the way I was feeling, I wished she hadn't. I just needed to move on and let her be. It was hard to do but I had to do it.

Tonight, Sameer was having a party, so Dasey and I decided to go together. I wasn't initially in the mood to go, but Sameer was my brother and I needed to try and keep my mind off of Nina. I knew a couple bitches, in conjunction with a couple drinks would suffice.

We walked into the venue and it was jumping already. It was a casual attire event, but everyone was still dressed to impress. I just wore dark jeans, a black thermal, black tennis shoes, and a black hat. I was not gonna pull out all the stops for these hoes.

As soon as I walked in, I saw Nina's pretty ass laughing and talking with some nigga and her home girl Madison. She had on a short red dress, and it was open from the middle and wrapped around to her side. I saw the side of her red lace G-string and licked my lips. Damn I missed fucking her little ass. Her hair was in a ponytail, and her baby hairs were slicked down. I saw she had on the watch, locket, and emerald diamond ring I bought her while we were together, and that gave me some hope. The guy grabbed her hand and kissed it, and my blood started to boil even though he'd just kissed Madison's hand too.

"Leave her alone," Dasey said to me and I nodded. Thank God he was here, because I was ready to snatch her ass up.

I walked over to my brother and Aubrie, and then greeted them. As soon as I sat down, Kiara sat in my lap. I looked to my brother and he shrugged.

"I didn't know you were coming," I smiled.

"You know I wanted to see you," she chewed on her lip. Aubrie shook her head at me, and then she and Sameer got up to dance.

"You look good tonight," I said as I scanned her.

"Thank you. So can I leave with you?" she asked. "It'll be just us without Gabriella finally."

"Of course you can," I licked my lips and she kissed my forehead.

Nina was paying no attention to me, so she hadn't noticed Kiara and I at all. At least I think she didn't.

An hour had passed, and I'd convinced Kiara to go dance and shit, so that I could watch Nina's every move in peace. Damn, what was wrong with me? I just wanted to go back to the old Yazir Willis that didn't give a fuck about any bitch.

My eyes followed Nina through the party for an hour straight, and now she was walking over to the bartender for a drink. I tipped my glass of Scotch up, and stared at her through the bottom of it. I heard Dasey laugh, so I knew he saw me.

"I'm about to go holla at Madison," he tapped my chest.

"I thought you were gonna leave that be for a while," I frowned at him. My eyes kept going from him to Nina, as I waited for his response.

"I was, but did you see her ass in that dress? I can't hold back anymore," he grinned and then skated over to her.

Just as I brought my attention back to Nina, some guy came from behind her and hugged her tightly. She giggled and then turned to face him, before throwing her arms around his neck.

I couldn't get out of my seat fast enough as I booked it over there. Dasey nor Sameer were around me to stop me from approaching her. As I got closer, the guy looked up from Nina, and frowned in confusion.

"Fuck is going here?" I folded my arms once I reached the two.

"Yazir, don't start," she waved me off and turned her attention back to old boy.

"Hey man, I'm Marcus," the guy stuck his hand out. I looked at it, and then brought my attention back to his face. "Oh damn, like that?" he bucked his eyes.

"Yeah like that, what you pushing up on my girl for?" I hissed and pulled Nina closer to me. She moved my hand off of her waist.

"What?" he furrowed his brows.

"For one, this is Madison's brother, and he's not pushing up on me. Secondly, I am not your girl," she twisted her face up. I felt like a psycho ass nigga right now, and I was slightly embarrassed.

"My bad bro, I-"

"It's cool," he said before kissing Nina's cheek and walking off.

Nina turned around to look up at me, and then shook her head in disappointment. She ordered a drink from the bar, as I tried to think of something to say.

"Baby, I'm sorry. I just saw you two and my mind went crazy," I apologized.

"Yazir, we are not together anymore and we will never be together again. Why don't you get that?" she squinted her eyes, confused by my behavior.

"Why you wearing the shit I bought you-"

"Because it's mine. I'm not gonna trash these expensive gifts just because I don't fuck with you anymore," she raised a brow and took her drink from the bartender.

"My letter, did you read it?" I questioned and cupped her chin but she snatched her face away as if she was repulsed by my touch.

"Yes I did, and it was a bunch of bullshit. If you loved me, you wouldn't have slept with that bitch. And while I was waiting on you to go on a trip? Really Yazir? I'm surprised you have any feelings for me at all, because if you even cared a tad bit about me, you would've at least done it on a different day," she replied, and a tear was sitting in her eye. I stared at her until it fell, and then reached to wipe it. "Don't touch me. I don't want you to ever touch me again," she gritted before walking away.

I was angry, furious, and enraged by her words. I walked over to Kiara who was talking to her friends, and grabbed her hand to lead her out of the party. As I was walking towards the exit holding her hand, Nina didn't even care. She saw me, but nothing on her face said that she was bothered, which in turn bothered the fuck out of me. Why did she have such a hold on me? Fuck!

Chapter Twelve: Matthew Jensen

Yazir was the fakest nigga on Earth right now. I swear I hated this nigga more than anything. I just knew once he started getting major bread he was gon' turn into a fuck nigga.

I'm his muthafuckin' blood, and he got the nerve to fire me? Then to make matters worse, he dragged his bitch ass back up into my crib trying to offer me some security job! I got four kids and two women depending on me, and ain't shit a security job can do for any of us.

Yeah, I hadn't been sending money down South but shit, how am I gonna provide when I have to get myself together? I told my baby's mother Robyn not to be asking Yazir for money, because I knew he would throw that shit in my face. Her ass didn't listen though, and now the nigga was mentioning it in front of Heaven and shit.

Not only that, but Heaven now knew that I was in another relationship down in Mississippi. I told her that Robyn was just my babies' mother, but she didn't believe that. He was fucking me all the way up.

Yazir and I grew up together somewhat. For most of my life I lived in Mississippi, and didn't move out here until I was twenty-two. Every summer though, growing up, Yazir and Sameer would come down to visit our grandfather, and the three of us were thick as thieves. We stayed tight for the longest, until Yazir's mother moved back down South. Once that happened, Yazir and his brother became so fucking money hungry, and didn't come down as much.

One year after his mom relocated, our grandfather Otis passed, and that only made Yazir go harder. He was determined to take care of our mothers, who heavily depended on grandpa Otis. Like he always said he would, he opened his own company after getting a patent approved for his flavored blunt papers.

I felt a tinge of jealousy once I started seeing his success, because I never believed he would do all the things he said; especially at his age. I just knew his business would flop and he would be broke just like me.

Over time, this nigga seemed to get richer and richer. His mentor in the drug game died, and he assumed position, which brought him major bread. Then Blue Dream shot off, and it was in every liquor store, even down in Mississippi. Then the club, and by that time I realized my cousin was that nigga, and decided to move to Los Angeles.

I hated seeing our mothers act like he was the best thing since sliced bread. Everyone always loved Yazir and Sameer. My grandpa would always brag about how much of a hard worker the two were, and that they would become something great. Whatever, they just got lucky in my opinion.

"So what's up, babe?" Heaven walked into the bedroom. She threw a stack of overdue bills in my lap, and then climbed back into the bed.

I met Heaven about six months ago, when she was working on Figueroa. I paid her for some pussy, and the shit blew my mind to the point where I had to wife her. She was light skinned, had long braids, a thick ass body, and a flat stomach.

"I don't even know, baby," I sighed.

Currently, we had no electricity, and I couldn't afford the rent on my condo. I refused to work that security job though. I felt like Yazir should've offered me a job at his corporate building for Blue Dream. Now that is how you're supposed to treat family.

"Why don't we get rid of your cousin?" She raised a brow and licked her thin sexy lips.

"What would that do?" I inquired.

"If we get him out of the way, you can take over everything," she shrugged and ran her finger down my chest. "Namely that booming drug empire," she grinned. Boy was Heaven bad.

"Nah, my cousin Sameer, or his best friend Dasey would take over," I shook my head.

I hated that Yazir put Dasey over me. He always said Dasey put in the work, and therefore deserved everything he was given. Sounded like some bullshit to me.

"Well we can get at all of their asses then," she smiled and caressed my face.

"What was you thinking?" I smiled back, liking the sound of her plan.

"I mean, you know where they hang out and shit. We can have them shot at or something. We just need them to all be in the same spot when it happens," she poked her lips out.

"Yeah, I smell what you're stepping in baby," I nodded. I felt happy as hell about this new plan. Just think of all the fucking bread I would have if I inherited Yazir's drug empire.

"But first, I think it would be good for you to make up with Yazir so he won't suspect anything if shit hits the fan. Also, it would be good for you to be on speaking terms in order to set him up properly," she kissed me. She was so fucking smart, and I loved an intelligent woman.

"See, that's why I love yo' ass. You're smart and sexy," I said before I smacked her ass.

"Yeah, and I'm gonna always look out for you, daddy. Once we get rid of those three niggas, you gon' be the king of Los Angeles," she chuckled and lit a blunt.

The King of Los Angeles, I repeated in my head. Damn did that sound good. That moniker would no longer be associated with my bitch ass cousin, but with a real nigga like myself.

"And you're gonna be my queen," I pulled her down and kissed her before taking the blunt. We were gonna be a fucking power couple, I could feel it.

***

The next morning around 9am, I decided to call my cousin up. Heaven was right in the fact that I needed to make up with him. Just in case the set up backfired, I didn't want Yazir looking at me. Also, it would be easier to know his whereabouts if we talked on the regular like we used to.

"Hello?" he answered the phone.

"What's up man?" I smiled as if he could see me.

"What you want?" he questioned with an attitude. I just wanted to square up with this nigga one time.

"Aye man, I been doing some thinking, and I want that security job you offered. It's time that I start being responsible for my kids and Robyn, you know," I explained.

"What brought this on? That bitch left you?" he quizzed just as Heaven started to massage my back. It took a lot for me not to blow up on his ass for disrespecting her, but there was a greater goal needing to be accomplished.

"Nah, I got rid of her," I looked at Heaven and smiled. She chuckled and then took a pre-rolled blunt from the ashtray.

"Well, I will think about it and give you a call back," his fake ass replied.

"What? I thought you said to let you know if I changed my mind? I need this job, cuz," I pleaded.

"Like I said, I'm gonna think about it and get back to you. That job may be taken, so janitorial work may be all that's left," he replied.

"Nah man, at least let me in the trap," I chuckled nervously.

"You definitely not working in the trap," he laughed as if it were a comical.

"Why not?" I frowned because I was insulted.

"The fuck you know about the trap, Matt? Do you even know how to use a gun?" he cackled and then I heard my cousin Sameer join him in laughter. I panted heavily, and Heaven rubbed my back to calm me.

"Yeah, you right," I scowled because he couldn't see me.

"I know I am. But I'll hit you later or some shit," he said and hung up before I could respond. Later or some shit? I was pissed as hell.

"Just take whatever he's offering baby. All we wanna do is get back in his good graces," Heaven explained. "So when he calls you, even if it's to babysit the crackheads that hang around the traps, just take it, aight?"

"I feel you. I can't wait to see them lowering his ass into the ground though," I glared at the wall as Heaven sat her chin on my shoulder.

"I know baby, soon enough." She kissed the side of my face and then handed me the blunt.

Chapter Twelve: Cherelle

I woke up in the Springfield Suites hotel room that Sameer had booked for me. I hadn't slept that well in I don't know how long. Having a soft warm bed, with a thick comforter on top of me was now a luxury.

I smiled and stared up the ceiling, until I remembered how my life had changed. I'd spent two years in jail for second-degree attempted manslaughter. Because Sameer paid for really good lawyers, I was able to get off with that charge, and a five-year sentence. I was released after two years, because I had served one while awaiting trial, and then because of good behavior the other two were waived.

My biggest problem though, is that while I was gone my husband had moved on to another bitch. I had no idea who the hoe was, but when I found out, I was gonna take her ass out just like the last one. I was gonna be smarter this time though. For one, I wasn't gonna get caught, and two she wasn't gonna make it out alive like the last hoe.

I'm sure you're wondering why I'm so hell bent on being with Sameer, when he said he didn't want me. It's simple; I cared more for him than he cared for me. It's always the same old story in most relationships.

We as women give a man our all, in hopes that one day he will reciprocate our feelings, when we know it'll never happen. We stick around until he leaves us for someone else, and we cry ourselves to sleep at night until we meet someone new, just to do it all over again.

Now see, a part of that was my situation, except I *was* gonna be with Sameer. Once he saw that no bitch of his would prosper, he would give up and be with me. He may hate me in the beginning, but once I showed him how good we were together, he would get over it.

I sat up because I needed to shower, brush my teeth, and then do some computer work. The first thing I bought with the money Sameer gave me was a laptop. This hotel had free Wi-Fi so it was perfect.

After taking my shower and running to Starbucks for a latte, I was ready to put in some detective work. First thing was social media. I looked Sameer and his brother up everywhere, but I found nothing on the usual sites like Facebook and Twitter. I then went to Instagram and found them quickly.

Sameer didn't post much, but when I checked the pictures he was tagged in, I saw most of them were with a girl. They appeared to be on vacation, in like Santa Barbara or something with a beach. I clicked her profile and bingo. Sameer was all up and through her shit. I laughed to myself because I found her so easily.

She was claiming my husband like they were meant to be or something. I became hot all over seeing that he was commenting sweet things under her picture like he was in love or something. He was supposed to wait for me, not go out and find a new girl. I would've thought he learned his lesson after I shanked the last skank.

Next thing I knew, tears were streaming my cheeks. I picked up my new phone and told Siri to call my husband. It rang twice and then went to voicemail, letting me know that he had hit ignore. I dialed again, he ignored, I dialed again, and he ignored. I placed another call, and he finally picked up. I wasn't gonna give up, so it was best he got it over with now.

"What Cherelle?" he barked into the phone. I knew he was angry but I didn't care.

"I found your bitch," I sniffled and wiped my cheeks.

"What?" He asked confused.

"Brie? Or whatever the fuck her name is!" I hollered. My heart was damn near beating out of my chest as the pictures on her Instagram flashed in my mind.

"You need to calm the fuck down, Cherelle. I can hear you fine so stop yelling. And what the fuck you doing snooping on my girl, huh?" he hissed.

"Oh, now you wanna be claiming her and shit? You weren't saying that during our calls or jail visits," I cried.

"I told you I was dating someone, I just didn't tell you who. Now Cherelle, tread lightly, because if you do anything to her, we are gonna have a problem," he threatened.

"You don't even know her like that, and you're already threatening me over her?" I shot up out of my seat. Oh, this nigga was a piece of fucking work!

"You look at it in whichever angle you like, but just know I'm not fucking around this time. Whatever you do to Aubrie, I'm gonna do to you," he stated sternly.

My heartbeat sped up even more, and my palms started to sweat because I was so angry. I wanted to kill her, but I knew Sameer did not threaten; he made promises. If I sliced this bitch up, he would kill me. I needed to find another way to get my man back.

"Well if I can't have you, then maybe I deserve to die," I smirked and wiped my dripping nose. Maybe going the sympathy route would do.

"Hey, whatever works for you. Just know if she dies, you die. No matter where you try to run and hide, I will hunt you down and gut you. I will dedicate the rest of my life to catching you and murdering you in the worst way possible. Now either you can live your life on the run, or you can get some sense, move on, and live normally. You be the God in your life," he said.

My shoulders moved up and down as I breathed heavily. I was so enraged it was ridiculous. How dare he speak to me in such a way? I was his wife! I am his wife! Me! Not her, or any other bitch he sticks his dick in, but me! Cherelle Jenee Willis! I am Mrs. Willis!

"Ahhhhhh!" I screamed and threw my phone against the wall. When it fell to the floor, I saw he ended the call, not even caring that I was having a melt down.

I started to trash the hotel room, because it was the only way I could release my anger. I broke lamps, ripped sheets, stabbed the couches, and wrote Sameer's name, along with some obscenities all over the walls.

Once I was too tired to continue, I grabbed my phone and purse, before hitting the road to speak with a couple accomplices that I may need in the next couple months. Shit was about to go down, I just needed to figure out how. I hope he let that bitch know he had a crazy ass wife in his life. If she wanted to be with Sameer, she was gonna have to fight tooth and nail for him.

Chapter Thirteen: Nina Joy

Tonight was my date with Seth. I didn't wanna go, but I felt it would help keep my mind off of Yazir. I didn't know why I was giving him such a hard time, yet being so lenient with Seth. I think it was because I loved Yazir way too much, and he had the power to hurt me. Where as with Seth, I didn't care for him that much, so he had no power over my heart.

I put my earrings into my ear, and then smoothed down my jeans. I had on skinny jeans, a black crop top, a red blazer, and black stilettos. I wore my hair down, with a deep side part, and my big earrings that Seth hated.

I heard a knock on my front door, so I grabbed my purse. I was now in my new apartment, and it felt good to have my own space. I opened the door, and there stood Seth. He looked nice, and his gray eyes sparkled upon seeing me.

"You look beautiful, Nina. I'm taking you somewhere nice so I thought you'd wear a dress, but it's fine," he chuckled nervously.

"Good, because I'm not changing," I said before closing the door behind me.

Long gone were the days where Seth could control my every move. Tonight he was gonna meet the new and improved Nina Jeffries.

We walked down to his car, and he opened the door for me. We pulled up to this restaurant named Sammy's in Manhattan Beach, and I couldn't help but pray for this to be over soon. I know I was supposed to be giving Seth another chance, but I wasn't interested at all. He'd already annoyed me by commenting on my fucking jeans.

We walked up to the hostess stand, and since it was pretty empty, they let us pick any table. We chose a rounded booth, where we could sit next to one another in the middle. His cologne was really strong though, and I was regretting that decision.

"I've missed you, Nina," he pushed my hair behind my ears. Seth was a gorgeous guy, and didn't look to be thirty-two at all.

I just smiled at his statement, because I refused to lie and say I missed him too. For some reason I felt like it was unfair to Yazir for me to say such a thing, even though he broke my heart.

"I still love you, ya know, and I wanna make us work," he said in a low tone as I looked at the menu. I could feel his breath on the side of my face.

"I think I'm too young for you, Seth," I sighed and stared at the drink menu.

"We're only what, nine years apart? That's nothing," he chuckled.

"I mean mentally. You need someone who is like you. I like to have fun, and wear jeans on dates sometimes," I looked into his eyes. His light skin was flushed. He took a sip of his water, to calm himself I guess.

"Nina, I'm trying here. I mean, you should be happy I'm even still interested after you ran off with that kid," he frowned.

"Kid? He's only two years younger than me Seth. And he doesn't act like it," I turned my lip up.

"Oh yeah? He couldn't even wait a year before he cheated on you sweetheart. You know why? Because that's what little boys do," he kissed my cheek as if he'd just said something nice.

"Thanks for the reminder, Seth," I exhaled heavily.

"Did you sleep with him, Nina?" I looked over at him, and his face was knotted up.

"Why?" I frowned.

"Because I want to know. The months that you were with him, did you fuck him?" he asked again and raised a brow.

"Seth, he was my boyfriend, what do you-" he put his hand up to tell me to be quiet, and then turned his attention back to the menu. I didn't have the energy to protest, so I did the same.

I couldn't imagine his reaction if he found out I sucked Yazir's dick, mainly because no matter how much he begged for me to do it to him, I never did. It wasn't like I hadn't given head before, because I did it to Phillip, but Seth just didn't make me wanna do it.

I was happy to see the waitress had come back to take our orders. I ordered some wine and a pizza, and Seth got some fancy salad and water. I missed the way Yazir would order fattening things with me. He would always say, *it's not what you eat; it's how much of it you eat. Everything is about moderation baby. Too much of anything is never good*. And clearly it was true, because Yazir had a way better body than Seth's carrot munching ass. And Seth was in the damn army!

"You know I have a ceremony coming up baby, and I would love for you to come with me," Seth said, pulling me from my memories of Yazir.

"Seth, I don't think that's a good idea," I responded dryly.

"Nina what the hell is going on? Is this because of that thug?" he frowned.

"No, it has nothing to do with Yazir, and he is not a thug. This has everything to do with the fact that I don't love you and I never have!" I blurted and then covered my mouth. He stared at me in disbelief, and laughed out of anger. I didn't mean to speak so cruelly, but he upset me by calling Yazir a thug.

"You never loved me, huh?" he raised a brow.

"Seth, I cared for you, and I tried to love you but you don't love me either. You wanna control me," I said.

"Lets go," he scooted across the seat so he could get out. I grabbed my purse and did the same, then followed him out to the car.

We got into his Infiniti, and he cranked it up before I even closed my door good. "Seth, I'm sorry," I said.

"Yeah, you are. You're a sorry little bitch, that's what you are. You aren't even worth my time, Nina. I don't know why I tried to bring a girl who was beneath me to my level," he scoffed as he buckled his seat belt, and then zoomed out. I refused to say anything because I didn't care. "Matter fact," he pulled over. "Get the fuck out of my car!" he hollered.

"Seth my house is far from here," I frowned.

"Get the fuck out before I break your face!" He screamed so loud his light face turned red. I pulled on the lever, and then climbed out of the car.

Here I was on the busy street of Sepulveda and Rosecrans, not knowing how I was gonna get home. I called Aubrie but she didn't answer, and neither did Madison, then I remembered they both worked tonight. I called my mom and got no answer either, which meant she was probably asleep.

"Fuck!" I shouted.

The buses didn't appear to be running, and I saw no taxis nearby. I took a deep breath, and then dialed Yazir.

"Hello," his voice came through the phone. I missed that voice so much.

"Hi, were you asleep?" I asked.

"Nah, what's up?" he quizzed.

"I'm stranded; can you give me a ride?" I inquired.

"Stranded," he repeated. "Where are you?" he asked.

"I'm on Sepulveda and Rosecrans, by Fry's Electronics," I responded.

"Be there in a little bit," he replied dryly and hung up.

I waited for about fifteen minutes, and then I saw his Range Rover hit the corner. I pulled on the handle, and when I saw him I got chills. He had on a grey jogger suit, and his tapered short fro was fresh from the barbershop. I inhaled sharply, not to breathe, but to smell his cologne I missed so much.

"Hello," I said.

"Sup," he exhaled and then pulled from the curb. "Where am I taking you?" he inquired.

"To my new apartment," I said and then directed him.

We didn't make any conversation, as "Proof" by Chris Brown played. The only time words were spoken, was when I was telling him to turn. He finally made it to my apartment, and I was thankful and tired.

"Appreciate it Yazir. Sorry for the inconvenience," I said as I hopped out. He nodded his head, and then I slammed the door and went inside. This was one hell of a night.

Chapter Thirteen: Yazir

A couple hours later...

I discover, discover I love her. Oh, I gotta get her back. I discover, discover, that I love her, oooh, that will get her back. I can't breathe, yeah. Can't breathe, can't breathe, yeah. Girl let me breathe again...

I sat and listened to Chris Brown plead for his girl to come back, and damn was I feeling these lyrics. I was still sitting outside of Nina's new apartment like a bitch. I couldn't believe she called me for a ride and that was it. She knew I was sick for her, and she had the nerve to hit me like I was a fucking Uber.

I ashed my blunt, rinsed my mouth with Listerine, and then popped a mint into my mouth. She was gonna take me back, and I wasn't taking no for an answer.

I got out and went up to her door. I beat on it loudly and repeatedly until I heard the locks being twisted. The door opened, and she stood there with a big t-shirt on and her hair disheveled. She could look beautiful wearing a trash bag.

"Yazir, what are you doing?" She wiped her eyes and pushed her long hair back. I walked in and closed her door behind me. It had to be about midnight by now.

"Nina, I love yo' ass more than anything, and I'm tired of living without you. I'm not doing this shit no more, and I'm not gonna allow you to move on and be with some other nigga," I said. She was about to speak but I stopped her. "Baby, I am sorry. From the bottom of my heart I am sorry that I cheated on you. I made a mistake, a big one. You have to believe that I love you Nina," I added and she was sniffling. She wiped her cheeks and then looked away. "We don't need to be apart," I said in a low tone before grabbing her face to make her look up at me. I kissed her lips gently, and then did it a couple more times. "I can't function being apart from you like this," I whispered as I pecked her.

"Yazir, you can't do this again," she sobbed.

"I won't. I promise I won't," I responded and kissed her lips some more. Feeling her lips against mine again was unreal at this point.

I kept kissing her until I reached what looked like the bedroom. I pulled her shirt up, and only stopped kissing her to get it over her head. She was naked under, and I dropped to my knees to kiss all over her stomach and pussy. Her scent was like the air I needed to breathe.

I laid her down, and spread her legs wide. I kissed her lower lips, and then began to suck on her clit. I missed doing this shit. I thought I would never taste her again.

"Uuhh," she purred as I feasted on her. She came quickly, but I was gonna keep going until I felt like I'd had enough to cure my starvation. "Aah, aaah, uuuh," she called out. I pushed one of her legs back, and stuck my tongue in her hole repeatedly, before bringing it up to suck on her clit some more. She exploded and I licked her clean like a human wipe.

I stood up and undressed as she watched me. As soon as I was naked, I climbed between her legs and kissed her passionately.

"I love you, Nina," I panted as my tongue danced with hers.

I loved the feeling of her soft body under mine. It was something I knew I would never experience again. I placed my dick at her opening and pushed in. Her pussy resisted me at first, so I put her legs in the nook of my arms. I pressed again, and I finally made it inside her. Her pussy was choking my dick and dripping wet. It felt good to know she hadn't let anyone invade my territory.

"Damn baby," I panted. "I miss being inside you," I said before sucking her lips.

"I missed you too," she cooed and scrunched up her pretty face.

I cupped one of her breasts, and then sucked hungrily on the nipple. I wound my hips into her while sucking, and she began to cry out.

"Did you give my pussy away?" I asked as I stared down into her face. She shook her head no, but I already knew the answer. She hadn't been touched since Santa Barbara by the way her shit was gripping me. "Fuck," I grunted and sped up. I began beating it up, and the sound of her wetness had my pelvis tightening up already. This shit was lethal, and the best pussy I had ever encountered. "Arrrggghhh," I growled as I shot my seeds up into her body. I bear hugged her torso, and then tongued her down. "I'll never hurt you again baby," I said to her as she caressed the back of my head. I let my dick sit inside her as we kissed for what seemed like an eternity.

"I love you, Yaz," she whispered, and it was like music to my ears. It was like hearing that oldie but goodie at a function.

Tonight I had finally gotten what I'd been begging God for, and I couldn't be more grateful. From now on, any bitch that even looked like a threat to my relationship was getting bodied immediately with no warning.

The next morning, I woke up to breakfast burritos and papaya juice, before having to get ready for church. Damn did I miss the good life of being with her.

Chapter Thirteen: Nina Joy

I was feeling good now that Yazir and I were back together. Shoot, I was feeling amazing! I did sort of think that I gave in too easily, but I loved him and I was tired of being miserable without him. I just hoped that he was serious about being faithful from here on out. I'll be damned if he has me out here looking like some fucking fool. If he tried to play me again, it would be over for good.

Today, Yazir was gonna meet my mother. She really didn't want to meet him, especially after Seth cried on her shoulder about me, but she needed to. I told her that Seth put me out on the street at night in order to convince her to meet Yazir and it worked. I wanted her to get to know Yazir so that she could see he was a great guy, and not some young thug who was stringing me along.

We pulled up to my mother's home at around 11am, because we were gonna go have lunch at Panera Bread. My mom loved that place, so we agreed to go there. I wanted her to be in the best mood possible, so I was gonna try and butter her up.

I called her on the phone to let her know we were here, and then a couple minutes later she walked out wearing a yellow sundress. Yazir climbed out of the car, and opened the backdoor for her, wearing his cute little smile.

"Thank you," she said to him as he helped her into his G-Wagon.

"No problem," he responded and then shut the door after her. I wanted to test her mood before he got in, so I decided to speak now.

"Hey Ma," I looked over my shoulder.

"Hi sweetie," she sighed and set her purse on the seat next to her.

Lord, please let this shit go smoothly, I thought.

We got to Panera bread in about fifteen minutes, and after we ordered we chose our seats.

"So how are you today?" Yazir asked my mom who'd been pretty quiet.

"I'm fine, how are you?" she cocked her head and sipped her drink.

"I'm good," he grinned. I could tell he knew she wasn't feeling him, but Yazir was a very ambitious person, so it was hard to knock him down to the point where he would stay down.

"So Yazir, why do you want to be with my daughter?" she asked and stared at him with a suspicious expression.

"Because I love her. I love her personality, and the way she carries herself," he responded and sipped his water.

"No, I mean when you first met her, you were very determined to be with her and I'm wondering why," she raised a brow. I shook my head at her, but she didn't see me because her eyes were locked on Yazir.

"Well, I thought she was beautiful. I was just really attracted to her," he shrugged and squinted his eyes.

"So you're all about the physical?" she folded her arms. *What the fuck mom? He just tried to tell you why he loved me earlier and you shut that down!* I screamed in my head.

"No, I'm not all about the physical, but you asked about when I first met her. When I first met her I didn't know her personality, but she was very attractive to me. I wanted her," he responded and I smiled.

"I see, and what is it that you do?" she quizzed even though I'd told her plenty of times.

"I own Blue Dream, I'm not sure if you're familiar-"

"Oh, the weed paper company, yes I've heard of them," my mother chimed in and gave him a fake smile.

"Yeah, and I own Dream Bar where Nina works, and ten Wendy's restaurants," he explained.

"Is that all?" she questioned just before the food was delivered.

"Yeah, that's it," he said and his face showed he was confused by her response.

"So you don't have any pharmaceutical jobs?"

"Ma! What the hell!" I scowled at her.

She was getting on my nerves trying to downplay Yazir like he was nothing more than a corner boy. Yeah he may have done illegal things, but he was a businessman too, and a successful one at that.

"Nina, I'm just trying to feel him out for you, because you're thinking with your heart and what's in between your legs! He's already cheated on you, what's next?" she pursed her lips, letting me know she was still angry about Yazir's infidelity. I pinched the bridge of my nose and exhaled heavily.

"I did make a big mistake, Mrs. Jeffries-"

"It's Ms. Roberts, I never married her father," my mom cut him off. She was so petty.

"I did make a mistake Ms. Roberts, but I love Nina, and I will do everything in my power to make her happy," he said. I was so delighted that he wasn't feeding into my mother's rudeness, and remaining respectful.

“Kind of early to be making mistakes already, don't you think Yazir?” She drank her lemonade.

“I totally agree, and that's my fault. But Nina knows that I love her and I wouldn't hurt her again. She made sure I suffered too,” he cheesed. I kissed his cheek and my mom scoffed.

All of her attempts to get him out of character did not work at all, and I was happy about it. One thing my mom loved was a respectful young man, so I knew Yazir would win her over in no time.

After our awkward lunch, we took my mom home. She did loosen up a bit halfway into eating, but she was still a bit standoffish.

“So what do you think, Ma?” I grinned because Yazir did such a good job handling her pissy ass attitude.

“He's very respectful, and surprisingly he seems to have genuine feelings for you. But we will have to see, sweetheart,” she gave me a half smile and kissed my cheek.

“Okay, goodbye Mom,” I hugged her and then went back to the car with Yazir. “She likes you but she doesn't want to admit it,” I leaned over and kissed his lips.

“That's a start I guess,” he chuckled. “You know I love you Nina,” he looked at me as he cranked up the car.

“I know,” I nibbled on my bottom lip, and then took his right hand into mine. I kissed the back of it as he pulled off from the curb.

I had never been this in love before, and I wasn't sure if it was a good thing or a bad thing. As the old saying goes, time will reveal.

Chapter Fourteen: Aubrie

I was sitting on my couch, chilling with Nina and Madison. We had so much to catch up on, so we just wanted to hang out and talk. We'd just come from having dinner at TGI Fridays, and I was stuffed like a Thanksgiving turkey.

"Do you have any tea?" Nina stood up. This bitch loved tea. I swear you could lead her into a trap if you tied a teabag to a string.

"Yes, I have some," I replied and Madison and I chuckled. Nina laughed too because she knew why we were, and then made her way to the kitchen.

"So what's been up? You've been too busy. I only see you at work, and you know Kelly's ass don't let me chill at the bar no more," Madison rolled her eyes referring to our manager.

"Just been working and hanging out with my man," I giggled.

"Your man must be one hell of a man, bitch. I haven't seen you smile that wide since Andre," she smirked.

"Andre was a waste of time, aight? Please do not compare Sameer to him," I pointed my finger at her and she threw her hands up in mock surrender. Andre was that bitch ass nigga who got a stripper pregnant while we were in a relationship.

Nina came back into the living room with a cup of hot tea, and then kicked her sandals off. "What y'all talking about?" she questioned.

"Hooking Madison up with Dasey," I shot Madison a look.

"Wait, what? I done already told you, I don't like people setting me up. Plus, that nigga has seen me plenty of times and he hasn't said nothing," she shook her head.

"He's seen you dancing up in the cage and that's it," Nina chuckled.

"So!" Madison shouted and grinned. She was so crazy.

"Is he supposed to climb up in there and get at you?" Nina cocked her head.

"I like men who are determined," Madison replied and we burst into laughter.

"No wait, what about at Sameer's party? He approached you then, and your ass was smiling and every damn thing!" I reminded them both.

"He sure did, so what happened with that?" Nina asked.

"Oh yeah," Madison rolled her eyes. "I mean he's cool, sexy as fuck, and got bread, but he told me he was just looking to have a good time right now and that's not what I'm trying to do," she sighed.

"Yeah I feel you," I nodded and so did Nina. My phone rang, and I saw it was my baby. "This is Sameer," I told my friends so that they could quiet down.

"Ooooh," they said in unison and I rolled my eyes.

"Hey baby," I answered.

"Sup beautiful, how are you doing?" he sighed. He sounded frustrated, so I knew something was wrong.

"I'm okay, how are you?" I questioned.

"I'm not doing too well baby, are you busy?" he quizzed.

"I'm never too busy for you," I flirted and he laughed. His laugh was so cute.

"Good," he chuckled.

"Can you come over here in like fifteen minutes? Bring a bag so you can stay," he said.

"Alright, is everything good?" I inquired.

"Umm, I will talk to you when you get here okay?" He responded, and his answer worried me. If he hadn't asked me to bring an overnight bag, I would be concerned as hell that he was gonna tell me he wasn't fucking with me anymore.

"Okay," I said and then we both hung up.

"About to get some dick?" Madison smirked and Nina grinned big as hell.

"I sure am, but he sounded down so I'm gonna go see what's up with him," I got up off the couch.

"Dang, I hope he is okay," Nina sipped her tea.

"Did Yazir say anything to you?" I asked and she shook her head no.

I walked to my room and started putting my bag together. About ten minutes later, I heard Madison call my name.

"What?" I yelled back.

"Someone is looking for you!" she shouted back.

I zipped my bag and then carried it into the living room. In the doorway stood a light skinned girl who looked like a younger version of Lisa Raye, except she was thicker in all the right places.

"Yes?" I frowned as I neared she and Madison at the door.

"Are you Aubrie?" she smiled.

It wasn't a nice smile though; it was a smile that said *I'm here to fuck your world up*. My eyes immediately went to her stomach to see if she was pregnant, but it didn't look like it.

"Yes, who are you?" I squinted my eyes and folded my arms.

"I'm Cherelle Willis," she responded.

"Cherelle Willis?" I cocked my head. Her last name alarmed me because that was Sameer and Yazir's last name. Nina came and stood behind me with furrowed eyebrows.

"Yes, I believe you're dating my husband Sameer," she giggled.

Chapter Fourteen: Seth Brooks

"Please Seth," Nina's mother Samantha begged me.

I had her tied to a chair in the garage. I was two seconds away from blowing her brains out, unless she could get Nina over here.

"Call her!" I screamed and she jumped.

"Please don't hurt my baby," she sobbed violently.

"Your baby is the one doing all of the fucking hurting! Now call her, I just wanna talk," I said and wiped the sweat off my forehead.

I was sweating hard as a muthafucka. I didn't know what the hell I was doing. All I knew was that I needed to get Nina back in my life for good. I had dropped by her apartment several times, but she was never there. She had blocked me in her phone, and I'd heard through the grapevine that she'd run back to that kid. I was losing my mind.

"You promise?" Samantha whimpered.

"Yes, I fucking promise." I shook my head and gave her a shit eating grin. She dialed Nina's number by sticking her hand through the ropes. I leaned down and tapped the speakerphone icon.

"Hey Mama," Nina's sweet voice came through.

I missed her so fucking much it was crazy. I hadn't heard her voice since I kicked her ungrateful ass out of my car! The nerve of her to sit and lie in my face saying she never loved me! I was the best thing that ever happened to that little bitch! *Calm down Seth*, I told myself. My phone buzzed, and I saw it was Maya.

Maya: *I just had the baby! Where have you been? I've been calling and texting you for days!*

She was gonna have to wait.

"Hey baby, can you umm-"

"Mama, why are you crying?" Nina questioned.

"Baby j-just come over here as quickly as you can, okay?" her mother sniffled and stuttered.

"Okay," Nina quickly hung up and I sat down on the floor.

"Seth, why are you doing this?" Her mother shook her head.

"Blame your daughter. I tried to give her everything and what did she do? She left me for another man! She didn't even have the common decency to sit me down and end the relationship! Then not only does she have him son me in my own home, but she comes right out and tells me she never loved me!" I laughed because I was so enraged. "That's why I'm doing this! She broke my fucking heart!" I screamed.

"I get that but she didn't mean it Seth. She was confused that's all. There are plenty of women out there for you Seth, just leave Nina in the past," she tried to convince me as her face became soaked.

"No! Now shut up before I splatter your brains!" I hollered.

We sat in silence until I heard Nina's keys in the front door.

"Mama!" I heard her yelling in the house. I walked into the house using the door that connected it to the garage, and stopped Nina in her tracks. I wanted to fuck her yet slap the shit out of her at the same time. Visions of her doing freaky shit with that boy infuriated me as I looked into her brown eyes. "Seth?" She frowned. "Where is my mother?" She questioned.

"She's over here," I pointed with a head nod. Nina rushed into the garage, and I slammed the door behind us.

"Seth, what the fuck?" she shouted to me.

"That's what I've been wondering," I said before pulling my gun from my waist.

"Seth, relax, okay. What do you want?" Nina panted.

"Oh baby, you should know what I want by now," I laughed loudly.

"What?" Nina asked as a single tear ran down her cheek.

"You baby, now all you have to do is come with me, and your mother will live to see another day. If you make this hard for me, I will kill the both of you right here," I explained.

"Seth, please," her mother begged.

"I told you to shut the fuck up!" I smacked her with the gun and Nina screamed.

"Seth stop!" Nina yelled, now crying like her mother.

I backhanded her with the gun as well, and she fell to the floor. Blood was spewing from her small nose, and she tried to stop it with her hand.

"Get the fuck up and let's go," I gritted.

She stared up at me, and when I cocked the gun she flinched. She quickly stood up, and I gripped the back of her neck as we headed towards the door.

To be continued...

CPSIA information can be obtained
at www.ICGtesting.com
Printed in the USA
LVOW04s2358130616
492399LV00029B/946/P

9 781530 856022